Also by Alyssa Hollingsworth

The Eleventh Trade

THE
INVISIBLE
BOY

THE
INVISIBLE
BOY

Alyssa Hollingsworth

WITH ART BY

Deborah Lee

ROARING BROOK PRESS
New York

Text copyright © 2020 by Alyssa Hollingsworth
Illustrations copyright © 2020 by Deborah Lee
Published by Roaring Brook Press
Roaring Brook Press is a division of Holtzbrinck
Publishing Holdings Limited Partnership
120 Broadway, New York, NY 10271
mackids.com

ISBN 978-1-250-15572-6

Our books may be purchased in bulk for promotional, educational,
or business use. Please contact your local bookseller or the Macmillan
Corporate and Premium Sales Department at (800) 221-7945 ext. 5442
or by email at MacmillanSpecialMarkets@macmillan.com.

First edition, 2020
Book design by Cassie Gonzales
Printed in the United States of America by LSC Communications,
Harrisonburg, Virginia

10   9   8   7   6   5   4   3   2   1

To the ones I encountered but did not see

Chapter 1

GIRL REPORTER UNCOVERS SCOOP OF THE CENTURY

Here's the scoop: A supervillain lives on my street.

And that's just the sort of breaking news I'm after.

The sun shines through my window for the first time in days. Before the rain can return, I grab my backpack and check my supplies: two pens (yes), three mechanical pencils (yes), Lois Lane press pass from Halloween (yes!), spare notepad (yes). Slipping the strap over my shoulder, I snatch my regular notepad from my bed and practice flipping it open. It swings to the next blank page with a satisfying *snap*.

I've known about the supervillain—alias Paddle Boy—ever since he moved here in January. Supervillains can generally be identified by a few basic signs:

1. Important, often rich family (bonus points if the parents are odd).
2. Scheming attitude.
3. Puts others (or their belongings) in danger.
4. Takes credit for stuff, especially stuff that someone else did.
5. Makes a big show of everything.

The very first time I saw Paddle Boy, I witnessed his senseless evil: wanton destruction of private property (signs #2, #3, and #5). I don't know what this guy has against canoe paddles—he fled the scene before I could catch him—but that's one of many questions I intend to get answered this summer.

Wonder Dog sits at attention by my door, her tail thumping on the carpet and her blue eyes sparkling with mischief. When I grab her leash, she hops up and turns circles. White and gray fur comes off her in a cloud. Australian Shepherds may be soft and adorable, but it would take infinite brushing to conquer their shedding. I blow some stray strands out of my mouth as I hook her leash to her harness.

"We've got a story to catch!"

When my Language Arts teacher, Ms. Thuran, asked me to write a headline-making, news-breaking article for the Junior

Journalists Contest in the fall, I doubt she realized I would snag a story as big as *this*.

Wonder at my side, I march down the stairs and to the front door. Mom is sitting in her home office, one room over, and she leans back in her chair.

"Starting your investigation already?" she asks. "You know, you're allowed to enjoy summer break a *little*. You don't *have* to hop to work the Monday after school gets out."

"I'm on deadline," I remind her. "And I have my first lead."

"Ah, I seem to have raised a career woman." Mom shakes her head but toasts me with her mug. "May your sleuthing be successful. I expect a full report when you get back."

I pull the door wide. "I'll see. Some of this might be confidential until publication."

"Have fun!" Mom calls after me.

"Yes, ma'am!" I reply in my best naval-officer-voice. As the door swings shut, I turn to survey my surroundings. Our lot looks like a badly cut piece of pie with the point at the street. On one side we have a neighbor, and on the other side there's a steep, briar-covered bank falling into the creek—we call it Little Hunting Jr., because it's a tiny tributary off Little Hunting Creek. The driveway cuts down the middle of our wedge-shaped front yard.

June occupies Northern Virginia with an attempt at humid

heat—but after my family was stationed in Florida and Mississippi, I have a high standard for "hot." And this, like most things in Virginia, is lukewarm at best.

Wonder pulls me down the steps to our lawn, sniffing around for the perfect place to pee. I'm not sure why she bothers searching, because she always goes in the same spot, but it gives me a chance to write in my notepad.

Date: June 17. Time: four o'clock p.m. Weather: Thick dark clouds and everything dripping, but no rain right now. Little Hunting Jr. has flooded into our yard, almost up to the pine tree where we store our canoe.

A canoe that's still short one paddle. We do have a single paddle left, but that gets really inconvenient out on the water. Dad says it's too much work keeping the canoe straight without the second paddler, and the current on the Potomac is too strong. Basically, Paddle Boy ruined everything.

After Wonder's done her business, I head toward the street. Paddle Boy lives five doors down from us, in an unassuming yellow house. This may not fit Supervillain Criteria #1 (rich family), but I'm willing to bet the simple everyday-man act is all part of his plan. Few would suspect this to be the choice hideout for a sinister mastermind.

Our street is basically a long narrow U, with a drainage

ditch in the middle. Water in the ditch passes through concrete pipes where Wakefield Street meets Stratford Lane, then flows down toward my house at the bottom of the U, where it goes through some more pipes and then to Little Hunting Jr. and finally Little Hunting Creek. I cross to the far side of the street, so I can start with a bit of spying, scope out the scene.

But before I pick a good scouting spot, Paddle Boy's front door opens. I tug Wonder close and duck behind a skinny tree.

Paddle Boy walks out.

He carries a big plate in his hands—I can't tell what's on it—and he's dressed in his normal I'm-just-an-innocent-kid clothes. It's the same kind of outfit he wears to school, an artful disguise our teachers never see through. They all think he's so great because he gets good grades and combs his honey-blond hair and says thank you to the bus driver. A classic bad-guy-pretending-to-be-good act. But I won't be fooled. What can he be doing out here?

He turns onto the street and begins walking toward me. Well—toward my house. I dive from behind the skinny tree to a slightly thicker one, though it isn't ideal cover. The water in the drainage ditch rushes like a river between me and him, gushing through the concrete pipes under the street ahead of me, then out into the ditch flowing fast toward the other pipes back near my driveway. Though they're nearly as big as I am tall, today the water almost completely fills them. At least with this barrier, Paddle Boy can't jump over to me and smash something else. Like my pencils.

Paddle Boy's gaze flits in my direction, and I press hard against the trunk. But Wonder—who has absolutely no common sense—wags her tail and gives a friendly bark.

I roll my eyes. There's no avoiding it now, so I spring out in the open. Across the median, I shout, "Hey! What are you doing?"

Paddle Boy startles and the plate flies out of his hands, scattering—cupcakes?—like grenades over the asphalt. His face turns redder than Superman's cape—villainous rage, I'd guess—and he runs the other way.

"Hey!" I call after him, scribbling notes without even looking at my notepad.

But right then, Wonder lunges.

If there is anything Wonder loves more than peeing, it is human food. And Paddle Boy just dumped a whole lot of human food for the taking.

The leash rips out of my hand. My notepad goes flying in the other direction. Wonder plunges into the water.

I run to the ditch's edge. "Wonder, no! Come!"

She keeps swimming, too keen to pay attention to me. Distantly, I hear a door slam—Paddle Boy has gone inside. A wad of branches breaks loose upstream, slicing through the brown water. It misses Wonder by a foot, racing on toward the pipes. I open my mouth to call again.

Wonder's head jerks to the side. Her leash, tangled in the branches, yanks her downstream, too.

I run along the bank. "No!" I shriek.

Now Wonder turns toward me and tries to move against the current. But she doesn't make any progress—the pull of the branches is too strong. The pipes are getting closer, and if she's sucked in, she could drown.

"Wonder!" I fling off my backpack and rush a few steps into the ditch, immediately soaked to my shirt. The water shoves me over, grabs my legs, and whirls them out from under me.

For a breathless moment, I kick at nothing, but then my toe catches on the submerged bank and I manage to push myself up the sloped side, sitting in the filthy mud. Ahead of me, the branches move faster as they near the big pipes. Wonder's head bobs under the surface and up again.

"No," I cry, voice cracking.

Then something rushes past my shoulder and splashes into the water.

A dark-haired boy just jumped into the middle of the rushing stream.

I don't know where he came from. It's like he appeared out of nothing, swimming toward Wonder.

I scramble to my feet and run to keep up with them. The boy grabs Wonder's harness. The branches vanish into one pipe. Just in time, the boy braces his feet on the pipe's concrete edge. He strains against the torrent, barely keeping himself and Wonder above the surface.

"Hang on!" I pull a large branch from the side of the road. I wade down the shallowest slope of the ditch and, careful to plant my feet wide apart, hold it out.

The boy fiddles with Wonder's harness, and then the leash comes off its hook and disappears with the branches into the pipe. Still struggling against the current, he shakes his wet, dark hair out of his eyes. He twists and grabs my branch. A scar below his wrist flashes in the pale sunlight. Now his red hoodie, soaked through with dirty water, looks nearly black.

I throw all my weight backward, dragging the boy and Wonder to the side of the ditch. When they reach land, the boy lets go of my dog, who bounds over cheerfully. I drop to my knees and hug her soaked, furry body to my chest.

"Oh my gosh," I gasp. My breath hiccups. "Oh my gosh, thank—"

I lift my head to look at the boy.

But he's gone.

I stare at the place he last stood.

What . . .

A shiver rushes down my spine, and I tighten my arms around Wonder. She smells like a wet dog, but I don't even care. She's safe. Paddle Boy's cupcake scheme didn't work—he didn't lure my dog to her demise.

"I'm glad you're okay," I whisper, blinking away tears. She bops my nose with hers. I can't help smiling. "We need to thank that kid."

I shift my attention back to the street. My notepad is lying on the asphalt. I grab it and my backpack, but my eye catches on a white piece of paper a few feet away.

Without hesitating, I pick it up, too, and turn it over in my hands. It's not paper—it's a photograph. In it, a woman about my mom's age stands in front of a bright purple town house. She's wearing jeans and a gray T-shirt, and her hands are clasped behind her. Her hair is frizzy and long, and her smile seems a little nervous. But she has kind—sort of sad—eyes.

I check the back again. In faded ink, there's a note: *Settled in the DC house. I have your room ready, whenever you decide you want to come. Love you, always and a day. Mom.*

The writing is a little smudged, but not too damaged. Which means it hasn't been out here during the recent rain—it was dropped, like my notepad, a few minutes ago.

It must belong to that boy.

I turn a full circle, trying to find any other sign of him. But there's nothing—I don't know the direction he went. The street is so wet, I can't even see any footprints.

I look down at the photo.

Just like there are signs that identify a supervillain, there are signs that identify a superhero.

1. A tragic family history (bingo! He's separated from his mom).

2. A talent at foiling schemes (like the cupcake trap for Wonder).

3. Rescuing people and their belongings (he saved Wonder's life).

4. Refusing to take credit, even for good stuff (he vanished without letting me thank him).

5. Most notably, a superpower (he vanished into *thin air*).

My pulse quickens.
Forget my supervillain story.
I think I've found a hero.

Chapter 2

HERO REMAINS ELUSIVE

Well, *found* might be putting it optimistically.

"I've never seen a boy like him on this street before," I tell Wonder. I brush mud off my cat-scientist leggings. My clothes cling to my skin, sticky and uncomfortable, but I haven't got time for that now. "How about you?"

She wags her tail unhelpfully.

Still. He must have been nearby when he heard my shouts for help. Which means he *could* live around here. In the year or so my family's been in this house, the only other kid my age that I've seen outside is Paddle Boy—and that's only because we ride the same bus from school most days. Everyone else seems to stay inside. Probably guarding national secrets, since as residents of Alexandria, Virginia, we're real close to Washington, DC.

The photo tucked safely in my notepad, I walk to the nearest house. It's regular brick with white shutters and a tidy collection of shrubs near the front entrance. I give the knocker a good strong *clang-clang*.

A man about the age of my grandfather opens the door. He blinks at me, as if a kid stopping by is the strangest thing he's ever encountered.

"Nadia Quick, girl reporter." I stick out my hand. He shakes it uncertainly. "I live down the street. I'm looking for a boy seen in the area ten minutes ago. He's about my age, wearing a red hoodie. Scar on his arm. Do you know him?"

The man blinks three more times. "No . . ."

"What about this lady?" I pull out the photo and show it to him. "Do you know anything about her?"

He looks more perplexed than ever. "Um. No. Wait, who are you?"

"Nadia Quick." I slip the photo back into my notepad. I don't have time for uninformed informants. "Thank you for your assistance, sir."

I run back down the drive with Wonder at my heel. One down, twelve to go.

At the next house, a mom juggling a toddler answers the

door. She hasn't seen the boy, either. I make my way around the loop of the street, skipping Paddle Boy's place—even if he had information about a superhero, he wouldn't talk willingly. His cupcakes are still squished on the road, but I keep Wonder far away from them. Someone answers every door—a girl wearing a college sweatshirt, a woman who asks if my parents know I'm out here, a man who's more interested in an overloud news broadcaster than answering my questions.

No one has seen or heard of this boy. If he lives on my street, he might as well be invisible.

The cloudy sky is getting darker. The air drapes over me, heavy. My stomach rumbles—it must be near dinnertime now. We'll need to call it a day soon.

I take stock of the final two houses: the one on the corner (whitewashed and gleaming) and the one next door (mismatched bricks that look like a jigsaw puzzle). As I watch, an old lady comes to the front of the jigsaw house. Her white-gray hair sticks out in tight spirals like a halo, and her dark skin makes her neon mismatched clothes almost glow. As I watch, she heads toward a birdhouse with a bag full of seed. I seize my chance and go straight to her.

"Excuse me," I call, smiling and waving. "Can I ask you a few questions?"

The old lady turns, her gray eyebrows lifting in surprise.

Then she laughs. "You certainly can, though I'm not sure I have many answers."

I describe the boy again and offer the photo for evidence. She listens thoughtfully.

"I haven't *seen* a boy," she says slowly. "But sometimes I hear someone working next door. Gardening, I think."

That sounds like a pretty boring way for a hero to spend his time. "So you do think there's someone over there?"

"Oh yes. I suppose . . . Well, it's a bit silly." She takes a handful of seed, but doesn't put it in the birdhouse yet. "I first noticed when my husband got sick. Whenever I could be spared, I came out to tend my garden. And one day I was just—so overwhelmed, it was as if nothing would work the way I wanted. And suddenly, there on the back patio, I saw a paper cup with lemonade in it."

I tilt my head, listening. This has some potential.

"It put me in mind of an angel." She starts to spread the seed on the little birdhouse porch. "It felt . . . a bit miraculous."

I write that down. "Has it happened again?"

She nods. "Four or five times. On hot days, or hard days, I'd turn around and find iced tea, or water, or lemonade. Sometimes a small piece of candy. Or, in the winter, three flower bulbs. Like someone is watching out for me. And then there was the time . . ." She hesitates, then takes a deep breath. "A day or two after my husband—passed, I realized I hadn't been in my garden for over a month, hadn't even really looked out the windows. I thought it would be ruined—full of weeds or eaten up by deer. I came out, and . . ."

She stops for a long, long pause, resting a wrinkled hand on her birdhouse's red roof.

I can't help prompting her. "And?"

"It was perfect," she says softly. Her eyes mist over and she smiles at me. "Not a single weed, and all the flowers happy and blooming. Just like it used to be, when the days were better."

My chest feels a little tight. Superheroes get a lot of press for saving cities and pulling babies from fires, but this is its own kind of heroic. It definitely sounds like the boy I'm after.

The lady clears her throat. "I would give anything to see the angel, but I haven't yet."

"Right . . ." I slow my note-taking. Does she think he is a *real* angel? Maybe this isn't the best source, even if she's the only one to give me any sort of lead.

"I wish I had something more . . ." A man comes out of her house and the lady's expression brightens. "Maybe my grandson knows."

"How's it going?" the man—her grandson—says as he walks up. He has dark skin, short black hair, and a trimmed beard. I'd guess he is a few years younger than my mom. He shifts an envelope into his left hand and offers his right to me, like I'm an adult. "Hi there. I don't think we've met? I'm James Wilson."

"Hi, I'm Nadia Quick." I shake his hand but glance at his grandmother. "Sorry—I should have introduced myself."

She waves off my apology. "Don't fret. I'm Mary Barton, but most people call me Mrs . . . Mrs. B."

Mrs. B's gaze grows distant, and she trails off into silence. Now that I think about it, I've seen an old man before, taken to and from the house in a wheelchair. He'd smile at me sometimes. I suppose that's the husband she talked about losing.

James touches Mrs. B's arm, and she seems to wake up again. She explains about my questions and her angel. He listens to it all with attention, even the more far-fetched bits. When she finishes, he squats to pet Wonder. "I haven't seen anyone, but I can keep a lookout."

"Okay. I live at the end of the street." I point toward my house. A loud rumbling starts from over there, and my mom comes down the driveway, pulling the recycling bin. I raise my hand to wave but Mom doesn't notice. I tell James,

"I'm on summer break, so I can come by and check for updates."

James glances at me, below my eye level now. "You live at that house by the osprey nest?"

"Yeah." Ospreys are huge water birds and kind of a big deal to Virginians. "I did a report about the babies for school last spring. They're pretty big now, though."

"Neat." He scratches his beard thoughtfully.

"James is a photographer," Mrs. B adds. "He's been documenting local wildlife while he's staying with me."

Photographer? That's not so distant from being a journalist. Lois Lane and Clark Kent had a friend named Jimmy, a well-intentioned but often silly photographer at the *Daily Planet*. I've never known a photographer before, but maybe this James could be handy to have around.

"You can come and see them," I offer. "There's a pretty good view from my yard. And I'll introduce you to my mom! She knows stuff about animals—well, about birds mostly."

"Oh—ah—Are you sure your mom won't mind?"

"No! She's right there." I point to her—now back up the driveway to get the trash can. "I just gotta check this last house and then I can bring you over."

"Well, then—I'll grab my camera." James stands and hurries inside.

Mrs. B laughs softly. "It was good to meet you, Miss Quick."

"You too!" While she turns to her birdhouse, I run across the yard. Wonder taps her nose against my ankle, which means, *Tired!* "I know, girl. This is the last stop, I promise."

I take the couple of steps to the whitewashed house's front door two at a time, then press the doorbell. It's a small button framed in shiny polished metal. On the other side of the wood, I hear a faint *ding-dong* echo through the house. But no one comes.

I wait a few moments, then lift the knocker—which gleams so brightly it could be gold instead of brass, I can't tell—and ram it down three times. Wait.

Nothing.

James comes out of his house, and I ring the doorbell again. This is the only house on the street where I haven't spoken to someone.

James calls to me, "You should try back in the evening."

"Huh?" I say as Wonder and I join him on the sidewalk.

"I've only been here about a week, but that place is totally abandoned during the day. She—that is, the owner—has parties almost every night."

She. My heart pounds. Does he mean the woman in the

picture? But this house is white and sterile, with none of the purple town house's quirky charm. Now that I think about it, I remember seeing a brown-haired lady greeting guests on the doorstep. She definitely isn't the mom in the photo, but that doesn't mean this isn't his house. It *does* have a high privacy fence around the backyard and thick curtains in all the windows. It could be a hideout. And lots of heroes have mentors disguised as butlers—like, Batman has Alfred and Iron Man has Jarvis. That could explain the woman.

James is still speaking, I realize a bit too late. ". . . this week. We'll probably go."

"Oh." I have no idea what he's talking about.

Mom's standing halfway down the driveway, apparently without noticing us, and is turned away talking to someone on her phone. Judging by her goofy laugh, I'm guessing it's Dad. I look down at the big camera in James's hand. "Do you only take pictures of wildlife?"

"Actually, I shoot weddings. Mostly. It can be fun." He shrugs. "My grandmother let me set up an office in her sewing room while I'm helping her."

"Helping her?"

He glances down at me, and the smile fades from his face. "My grandfather passed away a couple weeks ago. Cancer."

Oh.

"I offered to stay with her until . . . That is, she's going to have to sell the house and . . . it's difficult." He fidgets with the settings on his camera.

I'm not sure how to answer. No one in my family has died. I can't even imagine what it might be like.

"Look!" I spot the mom osprey landing in her gigantic nest. "They're home! Come on."

I cut away from the driveway and head directly to the creek, James on my heels. Even hurrying, it takes us a minute or two to cross the lawn. The swollen Little Hunting Jr. comes up almost to the grass, and then there's a peninsula between us and Little Hunting Creek. The osprey perches on a large nesting pole on the other side of the peninsula. "There. You have to get closer to really see it. Here—it's kind of tricky."

"Thanks!" James says when I point out a gap in the thorn bushes. When the creek isn't so flooded, there's a path here down to the water's edge. Right now, most of that is under-water. Wonder paws at the mud, but I pull her back before she can follow him.

I show James a tree he can use for balance. "Careful, though—that branch right there is rotting."

He smiles at me. "You sure know this area, Nadia Quick."

I beam. "That's basically my job. I'm the neighborhood reporter."

"Really? That's awesome."

While James uses the tree for support and lifts the camera to his eye, I flip open my notepad and jot some thoughts. There is a lot to update since my conversation with Mrs. B—even if there's not a whole lot to update about *him*.

Behind me, the rumbling starts again. I glance over my shoulder to see Mom finally continuing with the trash to the curb. At the same time, a car pulls into our driveway. My aunt Lexie slows to a stop, and a second later she steps out. I grin. She raises her hand to wave at Mom but walks toward me. Wonder spots her, too, and gives a great big excited bark.

James starts and flails.

I cry, "Not the br—"

He grabs the rotten branch for balance and it breaks, dumping him in the thorny mud. With a gasped adult-word, he's down. But he keeps one arm straight up in the air, holding his camera high away from the water and bushes and muck.

"Ouch," he says with a laugh. He sits up, and the mud slurps around his legs. "Thanks for the warning."

Aunt Lexie kicks off her heels and runs over to us. "What—"

"This is James Wilson. Photographer," I explain as quickly as I can. "I warned him about the branch, but he grabbed it anyway."

Aunt Lexie comes to a stop beside me and looks down in the briars at James. "Are you okay?"

"No harm done." James had been looking for an escape route, still sitting, but he glances up at Aunt Lexie and almost drops his camera.

"Camera!" I cry, and he straightens his arm.

"Thanks. Um—"

"Here." Aunt Lexie pushes her long hair over her shoulder, wraps an arm around the solid part of the tree, and extends her other hand. James rubs his muddy palm on his T-shirt and shifts to reach, and she grabs him by the wrist and hauls him out. The mud almost sucks off his shoe as he stumbles free. Wonder rushes to assess his condition while James opens and closes his mouth. Aunt Lexie starts to wipe tree bark pieces off her suit jacket, then gives up with a shrug.

"What happened?" a new voice calls. Mom jogs up to us and gets a good look at James. "Oh dear!"

"Is your camera okay?" I ask, barely keeping Wonder from tripping him again with her attentive sniffing.

"Yes—uh—" He looks down at it. "Yes, it's fine. Yes. Thank you."

I'm not sure if he's saying that to me or Aunt Lexie or Mom, because he's not really looking at any of us.

Aunt Lexie smiles at him. "Are you—visiting my sister?" But when she turns to Mom, her smile is tight. "I know you're making a big dinner, but I didn't know you'd invited . . ."

"Oh, I hadn't—" Mom starts to say.

"No, no!" He goes to put his hands in his pockets, seems to remember he still has his camera, starts to put both hands around it, then drops his dirty hand again to his side. "No, I live down the street. And I'd better get back home, actually. My grandmother will be—that is—not that I have to—I'm just staying with her for a bit."

Aunt Lexie is still smiling, but her eyebrows quirk up in a confused way. "Okay. Well, I hope you have a good evening. Sorry about the mess." She nudges me.

"Yeah, sorry," I chime in, even though technically I had nothing to do with it.

"Do you need a towel or anything?" Mom asks. Her gaze darts from him to Lexie. "You know, I could set an extra place . . ."

"It's fine! I'm good!" James backs toward the driveway. "Have a nice night!" Then he turns and hurries off.

Aunt Lexie watches, one hand on her hip and one coming to rest on my shoulder. "Miss Nadia Quick, where do you find these characters?"

I beam. "Oh, just wait until you hear who I met today!"

Chapter 3

PUBLIC DEBRIEFED

After a quick bath for Wonder, and a quicker shower for me, I rush downstairs in clean fox leggings and a big orange T-shirt. As I round into the living room, I ask, "Is Dad home yet?"

A moment too late, I realize Mom was in the middle of talking softly to Aunt Lexie about something. But she straightens and smiles at me. "He got held up at the Pentagon. Told us not to wait for dinner."

We all grab plates and food from the kitchen—Mom pausing to snap a picture of the dish en route—and then settle back in the living room. Aunt Lexie sits on the couch, curls her legs under her, and pats a nearby cushion. I plop down beside her. Even though she's changed into a pair of yoga pants and a comfy shirt from my mom, she still smells like fresh printer paper.

"I'm guessing we don't get your scoop until your dad's here, hmm?" Aunt Lexie asks. "You've got me on pins and needles!"

"News only breaks once," I tell them in a sage voice. "Everyone should be here for it."

Aunt Lexie sighs and asks me about summer break instead. I update her on the Junior Journalists Contest, and let her know I have a good lead for my story without giving away too much information.

Mom is busy typing on her phone. Aunt Lexie glances over. "Sis. Are you really posting a food picture right now?"

"Sorry," Mom says, not looking up. Distracted, she speaks slowly. "Just . . . adding some hashtags. An air force spouse . . . gave me this recipe, and I wanted . . . to let her know . . ."

Aunt Lexie and I share a look. In a loud whisper, I point out, "And people say it's the *kids* who are addicted."

"Hey—you both already ate some, right?" Mom glances up, apparently missing what I just said. "How was it? Give me a mini review."

Aunt Lexie indicates that I should go first, but I shake my head.

"No comment," I say, keeping to my personal goal of

staying off her blog as much as possible. Then I return to eating the (admittedly very good) tikka masala. I tune out the rest of the conversation—Aunt Lexie giving an answer and then the two of them talking about the blog, affiliate links, followers, etc., while Mom eats her now-cold food. Instead, I run the afternoon's action over again in my head. If the boy does live in that whitewashed house, I need to find a way inside . . .

Something loud scrapes outside—the garage door opening. Wonder leaps from her bed and runs down into the basement, barking. I grin. "Dad's home!"

A minute later, Dad comes into the living room, sweaty and smelly in his bicycle clothes. He puts an envelope down on the side table and gives Mom a quick kiss.

"Hmm, salty," Mom says.

"Gross!" Aunt Lexie and I chime at once.

"Sorry I'm late," Dad says, ignoring our commentary. "Admiral Sauron decided to drop an assignment on my desk at four forty-five, and it had to be done tonight."

"That's my husband, saving the world one piece of paperwork at a time." Mom pushes him gently away. "Go clean up."

Dad salutes and dashes upstairs, Wonder escorting him. We're barely done with dinner when he's back again, clean and in fresh clothes. He ruffles my hair and gives Aunt Lexie a side hug, then grabs his meal and plops down by Mom.

"*Now* will you share your news, Nadia?" Aunt Lexie asks, putting her empty plate aside.

I clear my throat and launch into the story. Paddle Boy's attempt at cupcake sabotage. Wonder almost drowning. A strange boy saving her life and then vanishing right in front of us. I pass the photo around and conclude with James Wilson's fabulous plunge into the mud of our creek.

"Hmm, so that was the nice-looking man in need of rescue?" Mom asks, glancing toward Aunt Lexie.

My aunt rolls her eyes.

"I don't think anyone could have saved him from his epic fall." I can't help laughing. "But he seems cool—other than that."

"All the boys on this street are particularly skittish today." Mom shakes her head. "Poor Kenny! I bet you surprised him, just up and shouting."

"Mom." I level a serious look at her. "Paddle Boy deserved it. He's evil."

"Your mom always has a soft spot for the bad boy," Dad says with a wink.

Aunt Lexie groans. It strikes me that everyone is paying attention to the wrong parts of the story.

Mom smiles and shrugs. "What can I say? I like complex

people." She drums her fingers on the couch cushion. "I wonder what he was doing with those cupcakes . . ."

"Baiting Wonder," I remind her.

"Ah. Right."

"Oh, hey." Dad goes to put his plate down and picks up a letter from the side table. He passes it to Mom. "This was in the mail slot when I came in."

Mom tears the envelope and pulls out a crisp white piece of paper with fancy silver lettering on the front. She flips it over. "Huh. It's an invitation to a house party." She scans the words and then lifts her eyebrows. "At 9000 Stratford Lane, that house on the corner."

My heart does a flip. James said there are parties almost every night. Maybe the superhero boy will be at this one.

"When is it?" Dad leans to read over her shoulder.

"This Friday at seven."

Dad asks, "Do we have to go?"

At the same time, I say, "Can I go?"

All the adults look at me. Dad chuckles. "Why? It's going to be adults complaining about traffic and politics."

"But this is an excellent opportunity for investigation," I point out.

When my mom looks a tiny bit worried, Aunt Lexie adds, "Discreet investigation."

"We should at least drop in, Richard—it's the neighborly thing to do," Mom tells Dad. She passes the invitation to Aunt Lexie. "You're staying with us while your apartment gets fumigated, right? Do you mind watching Nadia?"

"I don't need to be watched," I interrupt, sitting at my full height. "First, because I'm twelve. And second, because I can come with you."

Dad snaps his fingers. "I know. You disguise yourself as me, and I'll stay home."

"Not helping, Richard." Mom shoots him a look before she adds to me, "I think you'd be bored, Nadia. And anyway, we can't just abandon Lexie—and I don't want her to have to come socialize after a long work week."

Dad opens his mouth like he's going to make a smart comment, but Mom nudges his arm and sharpens her look from Unamused to Definitely Annoyed.

"You and Lexie can have a pj's marathon of *Superman*," Mom offers, turning back to me with a peacemaking smile. "I'll order pizza."

She does know how to tempt a person, but my mission is more important. However, I know it's useless to argue with Mom now. I have to be clever to get her to budge.

"It's settled, then." Mom grabs a pen from the coffee table

and ticks a box on the invitation. "I'll put down me and Richard, and you two can stay in."

While Mom keeps talking to Dad about the party, Aunt Lexie leans over and whispers in my ear, "You're still planning to investigate, aren't you?"

I glance up, worried she might rat me out to my parents.

But Aunt Lexie winks. "I'm in. I want to meet this superhero— Hold on, does he have a name?"

"Not that I know."

"As his first contact with the press, you get naming rights, I believe."

It's a good point. After all, in some versions of the comics, Lois Lane is the one who originally coins Superman's name. I run through everything I know so far—tragic past, water-saving abilities, vanishing . . . No one has seen him in this neighborhood, except me. It's almost like they *can't* see him.

The perfect name springs to mind.

"The Invisible Boy."

Chapter 4

INVESTIGATION ONGOING

That Friday of the party, I tug on a dress covered in Superman logos and pull my hair into two loose braids. I can hear Dad opening the door for Aunt Lexie, so I head down to join them. He's in a sort of casual suit, and my aunt looks fabulous in a yellow dress that swishes around her knees when she turns.

"You really don't have to stay in your work clothes, Lex." Then Dad sees me. He shifts Aunt Lexie's overnight bag into his other hand and narrows his eyes. "Wait, why are you all fancy?"

Aunt Lexie gives me a thumbs-up. "Excellent choice."

"Where's Mom?" I ask, right as the bathroom door by the dining room swings open and Mom walks out.

"Sorry," she says. Her skin's kind of greenish, and she gives me and Aunt Lexie a confused look. She's wearing a loose black dress. Very boring. To Dad, she says, "I think something at dinner disagreed with me."

"Are you up for going?" Dad asks, brushing back her hair.

"Absolutely." She loops her arm through his. Then she turns to us. "You're awfully dressed up for a *Superman* marathon."

"We're coming with you," I announce. I have been working on my argument all week, to find the one that would make Mom relent. "As a good neighbor, it is my responsibility to join my family in meeting our community."

"In other words, you still want to investigate," Mom says.

I hesitate, then shrug.

Mom shakes her head. "Well, if you're that set on it, fine. I don't think we'll stay too long anyway."

Dad brightens. "That's good to know."

Mom ignores him. "You sure you don't mind, Lexie?"

"Nope." Aunt Lexie smiles. "I'm curious about what we'll find."

Dad passes me Aunt Lexie's bag, and I run it upstairs to the guest room. While I'm there, I make a quick check to be sure Wonder Dog has her comfort animal—a stuffed squirrel—and plenty of water. Then I hurry after the adults so Dad can lock the door behind us.

Outside, the cool wind brushes against my bare legs. I wish I had worn leggings under my dress. It's barely seven p.m., and the sun hasn't set yet. The air shimmers with clouds of gnats as we head down Wakefield Street. Aunt Lexie takes my hand and swings it, making the bracelets on her arm jingle.

"So, have you had any luck in your investigation of the Invisible Boy?" she asks me.

"No," I admit. "I haven't seen him. Paddle Boy's been quiet, too. He seems to know that I've got a new ally, because whenever he sees me, he goes back inside his house."

Aunt Lexie smiles. "And I suspect there has been a drop in criminal activity?"

"Some new litter in the median, but I suppose that can't be directly linked to him." I frown. "It's been a pretty boring week."

"Don't be too disappointed. I'm sure things will get hectic again before you know it." Aunt Lexie sighs. "I would give anything for a boring week now and then."

Aunt Lexie works in Washington, DC, on something to do with traffic. You can't get anywhere around here without traffic, so someone's got to deal with it, I suppose. I'm not sure exactly what Aunt Lexie does, but I try to sound like I know what I'm talking about when I say, "Traffic been bad?"

Aunt Lexie rolls her eyes. "Don't get me started. It should've taken thirty minutes to get to your house today—not an hour and a half!"

I nod sympathetically while flipping my notepad open with my spare hand. We're getting close to the whitewashed house on the corner, and I need to focus on my objective. Cars are parked along the street out front, and the windows shine bright and cheery. As abandoned as it seemed when I knocked earlier this week, it's bursting with life now.

A woman with brown hair stands by the open door, welcoming people. She has the typical business-lady DC haircut (straight and exactly framing her jaw) and smiles with commercial-style white teeth. Her quietly commanding presence would make her an excellent butler-mentor. I make a note.

"Hello!" she says as we approach. She holds out her hand. "I'm Candace Goldenberry. And you must be . . . ?"

"Karen Quick," Mom answers, shaking her hand. "And my husband, Richard; daughter, Nadia; and sister, Lexie."

"So nice to meet you." Candace shakes all our hands in turn. Her manicured nails prick my skin. Even though

Candace has on heels, she isn't very tall, and Aunt Lexie stoops slightly to greet her. I don't think my aunt even knows she does it.

"I'm so happy you all could come," Candace continues once everyone has been greeted. She waves us toward the hallway, her gaze on the next family. "Go ahead and make yourself at home. Drinks and snacks are in the kitchen."

Mom and Dad lead the way in, me and Aunt Lexie following. Stylish adults mill around the living room, wearing slacks and button-ups and blazers and dresses. I examine the small crowd, half listening as Mom starts to introduce herself to some of the guests. She passes Dad and Aunt Lexie glasses of red wine but takes water for herself.

I don't see anyone my age. And I definitely don't see a boy/superhero.

Though, if he *does* have the power of invisibility, spotting him isn't going to be easy.

James Wilson stands at the other side of the room with Mrs. B. Mrs. B's talking to another lady, but James looks over at me and my family—and keeps looking. I wave, but he doesn't seem to notice. I glance over my shoulder. He's looking at Aunt Lexie.

Hmm.

People have gathered closer to speak with Mom, and she's

launched into blog-talk. Dad stands at her elbow, eyes a little glazed as he listens to the jokes she uses for catchy first impressions. Aunt Lexie smiles and laughs.

I glance across the room again. James sees me when I wave this time, and he smiles back. He leans over to Mrs. B and says something, and then the two of them start coming toward us.

I tap Aunt Lexie's elbow, wanting to get her away before Mom starts on stories of the military spouses she's interviewed.

"Aunt Lexie," I whisper, "come meet James's grandma. She's really cool!"

Aunt Lexie turns away from my mom's audience. "Oh, okay."

I pull her toward the patio door, so we'll meet James and Mrs. B a convenient distance from my parents. Aunt Lexie smiles politely at them, and James grins in a super-goofy way.

Hmmmm.

"Hi," James says as soon as they get to us. "How are you?"

"Doing well." Aunt Lexie shifts her gaze to his grandmother. "And you must be Mrs. B? Nadia has told me about you."

Introductions are made. Mrs. B asks questions about Lexie's work, and she mentions trafficking and DC, and

Mrs. B starts talking about her garden and her job as a counselor before her husband got sick . . . James stands to one side, attentively listening to them both. Well, *listening* to them both but mostly *watching* Aunt Lexie.

HmmmmMMMMM.

Aunt Lexie is single.

James is nice. Clumsy, but nice. And he didn't mention a girlfriend.

Maybe this is another scoop, right under my nose.

"What about you, James?" I cut in, trying to get him to stop standing there like a speechless weirdo.

"Oh—I—you know, I do wedding photography."

Aunt Lexie nods. "I'm sure that must be a handful."

"It is, sometimes," he agrees. This would be the perfect time to talk about wedding disasters. Based on the movies, I imagine at least half the ceremonies end with someone running through the door declaring "I object!" But instead of sharing a story that would be conversation gold, he opens and closes his mouth and says nothing at all.

For a moment, no one talks.

Then Aunt Lexie goes back to asking Mrs. B about her old job.

This scoop is going nowhere fast.

A steady stream of people have trickled in since we arrived, and out of the jumbled voices I suddenly recognize one in particular. A creaky, slightly-too-loud voice. A voice that personifies pure evil.

I lean away from Aunt Lexie and try to peer around the adults between me and the hallway.

Suddenly the crowd shifts. He sees me and cuts off mid-sentence.

I narrow my eyes.

Paddle Boy is here.

Which, with any luck, might mean the Invisible Boy is not far behind.

Chapter 5

THE SEARCH CONTINUES

Paddle Boy approaches. I flip open my notepad, just so he knows this conversation will absolutely be on the record. He stops in front of me and crosses his arms over his polo shirt. His mom or someone probably helped him spike his hair with gel, because it is looking particularly dumb tonight.

"Hi, Nadia."

I nod, civil. "Paddle Boy."

"My name is Kenny."

"Sure it is, sure it is." I poise my pen over the paper. "Are you here to sniff out the new hero on the block?"

"New hero . . . ?" He blinks at me like I'm speaking another language. "Seriously, could you be any weirder?"

I maintain enough professionalism not to outright roll my eyes. "I'm talking about the boy who saved Wonder Dog. People call him the Invisible Boy."

"Wait—someone saved your dog? From what?"

This feigned slowness is not actually that unusual for Paddle Boy. We've talked a total of ten times since the paddle incident, and he always acts thick. "Right. From *you*."

He lifts one eyebrow. It is super annoying that he's figured out how to do that. I still haven't mastered full eyebrow control. "I don't know what you're talking about."

"Oh, I think you do."

For a few long seconds, we say nothing. I stare at him. He stares at me. I keep my hand closed firmly around my pen, so he won't be able to snatch it and break it. The crowd—and the possibility that the Invisible Boy might be nearby—is good insurance that he won't try something more dramatic. And even if the Invisible Boy didn't come to stop him, I have my own forms of defense.

Where is the Invisible Boy, anyway? Shouldn't he have shown up by now?

Though maybe he is here. Just invisible.

"I heard that your mom is going to make a big announcement in a few weeks," Paddle Boy says. "Do you know what it's about?"

My grip tightens and my spine goes rigid. "I told you to stay off her blog."

"I didn't go on her blog—my mom's super curious and she wanted me to ask. That's why she had me bring—well, I was supposed to bring over those cupcakes. To be *nice*. Until you ruined it." In a tone of dismissal that might be a tad disrespectful, he adds, "It's not like I *intentionally* follow your mom's blog for military spouses."

But his eyes shift away as he says it. He's a liar, through and through.

Here's the thing about being a sleuth when your mom is a viral blogger: Sometimes you end up in her updates. Sometimes the updates are totally about you.

And sometimes, supervillains use that blog to gain information they should never, ever have.

I snap my notepad shut. Paddle Boy is giving me nothing new to work with, and he is just as insufferable as always. Without even saying goodbye, I turn on my heel and march to the closest exit—a sliding glass door that opens to the backyard. Aunt Lexie is still talking to Mrs. B, James is still failing to talk to Aunt Lexie, and my parents are still surrounded by neighbors. No one notices me leave.

Outside, the sun has set and the air has gone from cool to downright chilly. I rub my arms, looking around. Fairy lights strung from trees lead down paths deeper into the yard. Other guests linger on the patio, some people sitting on nice matching furniture around a comfy firepit. The guy who was listening to news during my neighborhood survey is now explaining very loudly about some breaking story. Politics, I think. The lady he's talking to keeps trying to respond, but he just talks louder.

Wrinkling my nose, I cross the patio and head down one of the paths. The mulch softens my footsteps, until I hardly make any sound at all. Smooth round stones mark the border of the trail. Soon, the noise of the party fades. The yard goes back pretty far—much farther than I would have guessed. Candace must be *way* rich to have this big of a yard.

More important: This big of a yard presents a new possibility. Because it's perfectly sized for a secret hideout.

I stop to peer beyond the lights. My eyes don't want to adjust to the darkness, so I glance around to make sure no one is nearby. Then I step over the rocks and slip into the grove of trees.

At first, everything looks the same—trees with cleared ground beneath, so empty you'd hardly even find a root to trip on. Bushes and flowers weave around trunks artfully, but in the dark I can't see much detail.

Then, among the shadows, I spot something unusual. Squarish. A shed.

If anything screams Fortress of Solitude, this does.

Maybe there's a secret elevator inside. One that drops below ground to a full lair of high-tech equipment and costumes. An invisible scooter, maybe? Or jet? Wonder Woman has an invisible jet.

Holding my breath, I step around bushes and feel for a way in. Rough wood rises under my fingertips, coarse enough that it might give someone a splinter (perhaps a security measure for the fortress?). I find a cold metal latch. It lifts easily, and the door opens without even a squeak.

I wait for motion-sensor lights to flicker on. A secret wall to slide back. A robot voice to ask for a password.

But the shed remains dark and silent.

I fumble for a light switch, but there isn't one, so I just have to guess at the different shapes. Gardening stuff. Bags of soil. Rakes. And amid the sharp angles of tools and shelves, I don't see anything that looks remotely like a boy. I poke at the walls blindly, but have no luck there, either—I can't find a button that would make the floor turn into a slide and dump me in a real, actual hideout.

"Hello?" I ask the air, figuring it's worth a shot. After all, he is invisible.

Nope.

The shed is completely still.

Exhaling, I slip out and shut the door softly. This night is not going well for my investigation. On my way back to the path, I drag my feet. Maybe the Invisible Boy doesn't have anything to do with this house. Mrs. B said she *thought* an angel was around here, which could have been the boy, but she's old and clearly confused.

My shoe catches on something and I fall, yelping in surprise. My knee hits one of the rocks on the edge of the path, and pain shoots up my leg. It takes a full five seconds before I can inhale again.

Cautiously, wincing, I turn my leg toward the dim light. My knee is dirty and—I think—bleeding a little.

Sighing, I shift to see what tripped me.

It's a bundle of cloth.

A sweatshirt?

My heart stutters.

I grab it. The path lights illuminate the shapeless lump in my hands. It's a hoodie—an unusually heavy red hoodie. The thick fabric frays around the hem. Along the right sleeve are random, scattered holes. They're as small as the tip of my pinky, with hard, dark edges. The whole thing smells like boy sweat.

The Invisible Boy wore a hoodie just like this when he saved Wonder Dog.

I shift the weight between my hands. Something slides around in the zipped pockets. I open them and pull out whatever I can grab—a protein bar, small flashlight, and two wrinkled photographs. I click on the flashlight and wince at the sudden white-blue beam. I shine it at the first picture, where there's a woman with a toddler on her shoulders—the same woman who's in front of the purple house, but here she's younger and her hair is less frizzy. Nothing's written on the back.

I flip to the second picture and gasp. In this, a golden retriever sits and stares at the camera—and beside it, in a blur, is the very edge of the outline of a boy. The left side of his body is just about there, but the rest has vanished.

My breath hitches in my throat. The Invisible Boy.

I return the stuff to the pockets and zip them closed again, almost shaking with excitement. He's here. I know it. A superhero wouldn't leave something like this lying around—that would be like Clark Kent forgetting his glasses, or Superman discarding his cape.

And if he's here, I'm going to find him.

I push myself to my feet. My knee stings and throbs, but I ignore it, rushing back into the house with the hoodie folded over my arm. No parents, aunts, or guests notice. I send up a prayer of thanks to Lois Lane, patron saint of snooping.

Paddle Boy is waiting for me right inside, but I lift my chin and walk past him. He follows me anyway.

He asks pointedly, "What are you doing?"

"Nothing." I snap my notepad open and weave between adults toward the hallway. Candace is talking to my parents, and James is handing Aunt Lexie a new a glass of wine. I continue to the hall and pause to take stock of the layout. Just off the front door is a living space with a bunch of white furniture and white carpets. A few guests are chatting there. On my right is a staircase to the second floor.

I head up the stairs.

"I bet you aren't allowed up there," hisses Paddle Boy from behind me.

I spin around on the step. "I'm looking for a bathroom."

"Well then, there's one by the kitchen." He frowns. "Why are you sneaking around?"

"I'm *not*." I point down at my hurt knee and embellish the truth with some creativity. "I need a bathroom *with a first aid kit*, and the one down here doesn't have one. It's fine, Candace gave me permission."

"Right." He looks skeptical. "Sure . . ."

I don't wait to convince him. I hurry up the stairs. My

knee hurts with every step, but it doesn't slow me down. Paddle Boy may be easily confused, but it's only a matter of time before he tries to interfere with my investigation. I've got to find the Invisible Boy first.

On the second floor, I take a quick inventory.

The master bedroom is open—I can see a neatly made bed with a white quilt folded over the white comforter. There's another door, also open: a bathroom. I turn away from that. Two more rooms on this hall. Neither has a light shining under the door.

I go for the nearer door first. I ease the doorknob until the latch clicks. Inside, streetlights shine through a window. It's a guest bedroom. The bed is frilly, with flowery covers and lots of lace—something no boy (or kid of any sort) would be caught dead sleeping in. On the wall is a canvas painting of a deeply boring white rose.

This is not the Invisible Boy's room.

I dart to check the next room. Inside, there's a white desk with a Mac computer and papers stacked neatly on one side. A white bookshelf with color-organized books rests against the wall. Nowhere to sleep. An office, not a bedroom.

Carefully, I close the door, playing the layout of the house through my head. Downstairs: formal living room, kitchen, bigger living room, bathroom. Upstairs: two bedrooms, an office, another bathroom. But nowhere a kid superhero might live . . .

The basement! Possibly the most obvious place in the whole house, and I almost missed it!

Feeling kind of dumb, I slip back down the stairs. Paddle Boy is in the big living room, his back to me, and adults are still chitchatting away. In the kitchen there's a second door next to the bathroom. I hope it's the basement.

I pull the door open. Stairs lead down into darkness. Bingo!

I fumble for a light switch but change my mind. Light might attract attention. Straightening my shoulders, I take the first step and shut the door softly behind me. I dig around in the hoodie pocket for the little flashlight, and I hold it in my left hand with my notepad in my right. I feel for the first step with the toe of my shoe before I move. My footsteps are quiet and perfectly stealthy. But I don't want to startle the Invisible Boy. It's not a good idea to sneak up on superheroes.

I click on the flashlight and move down the next few steps quickly. Into the silence, I whisper, "Hey, um—" I can't exactly call him by his superhero name, because he doesn't know it yet. "Um—anyone down here?"

No response.

"Hey, I have your picture." I jostle the hoodie, draped over my left arm, so the stuff in the pockets knock together. "And your hoodie."

In the beam of light, I can see the general shape of random objects. A chair. Some boxes. A table beneath the windows. But no person. I can't hear anyone else even breathing down here.

I put my foot on the floor of the basement. Light explodes behind me.

Blinded and surprised, I drop the Invisible Boy's hoodie and flashlight and only barely manage to keep ahold of my notepad. I whirl around and blink, eyes watering. Two shadows stand at the top of the stairs.

Paddle Boy.

And my mom.

Flake-flipping snow fairies . . . !

"Nadia?" Mom asks. Her face colors. "This isn't—Nadia, come up here *right now*."

I climb the stairs slowly. My thoughts spin in circles. The basement was my last option. This can't be the Invisible Boy's hideout. Even if he is being invisible right now, he's got to have somewhere to sleep.

Paddle Boy moves back to make room for me in the hallway. I channel all my frustration into my face as I look at him. If I had laser vision, he'd be toast. He shakes his head at me and shrugs.

"Thank you, Kenny," Mom says.

My jaw all but drops on the floor. "Mom!"

Mom waves Paddle Boy back toward his mother. He pauses long enough to give me a slight smirk and then goes.

Before I can remind my mom not to thank known supervillains, Candace comes down the hall. "Everything all right here?"

"Yes, my daughter just got lost trying to find the bathroom," Mom says with a pointed look.

"Ah. Well, it's certainly not in the basement!" Candace laughs and reaches around me to close the door. When she leans close, a faint scent of cigarette smoke wafts under her perfume. Before she lets go of the door handle, she gives it a push, like to make sure it's firmly shut. To me, she adds, "You're one door off."

"I think we should be heading out anyway," Mom says, a blush still coloring her face. "Thank you so much for the invitation to your home. It's lovely."

While they exchange goodbyes, and while my mom gets Dad and Aunt Lexie, and while we walk back to my house, and while my parents lecture me about not sneaking around other people's houses, my thoughts zip right back to the

Invisible Boy. It's not until I get up to my room that I realize I left the hoodie in Candace's basement. Other than the original photo of his mom at the purple house, my primary evidence of the Invisible Boy's existence is gone. And I'm no closer to finding out where—or who—he is.

Chapter 6

SECRETS SPREAD TO NEW TERRITORIES

The weekend passes without much happening, mostly because I'm grounded, banned from walking Wonder (Dad does it) or hanging out with Aunt Lexie (even though she's here until Sunday night). My parents believe that snooping around a neighbor's house during a party is not an "appropriate" way to investigate. They don't offer any useful suggestions for how *else* I might go about it, so I think that their input lacks some practicality. I use the opportunity to throw myself into my work—jotting down floor plans in my notepad, recording every last detail I can remember about the Invisible Boy, and trying to train Wonder Dog to crawl silently beside me for future stealth missions. Mostly Wonder just ends up nibbling at my hair instead.

On Monday, newly freed and more determined than ever to get to the bottom of this story, I take Wonder Dog on her usual afternoon walk. The street is quiet—like usual. I keep my gaze on the whitewashed corner house as we move down the street. Maybe the Invisible Boy doesn't live—or, at least, sleep—there. But he left his hoodie, which means he must be nearby. My research confirms a superhero would return for such an iconic piece of their costume.

Wonder Dog yanks on her leash, trying to get at something in the center of the dried-out drainage ditch in the median.

"Heel," I command, tugging her back beside me. She huffs and stops pulling so hard, but still stares down there at a scrap of chicken. It's on top of a brick.

A corner of paper peeks out from beneath the brick.

I tie Wonder's leash around a tree trunk, so she won't eat the chicken. It could be another Paddle Boy–concocted human-food trap. Once she's secured, I slip and slide down the edge of the ditch, rocks and leaves falling away under my feet. At the bottom, I kneel, nudge the chicken off, and lift the brick. The piece of paper is crisp and folded. It hasn't been out here long.

I open the paper with one hand. Something is scribbled on it—the handwriting is almost unreadable. I squint.

"Please leave my photo here."

My heart just about stops. The Invisible Boy.

I look back at the brick. One side is painted white. A side that could be faced out, if it was part of a wall. The white-washed house is almost directly behind me. Did he come from there?

I have a thousand—no, a *million* questions.

But one thing's for sure: I'm not leaving his photo for just anyone to come and grab. He should know better, with Paddle Boy living right there. This sort of sensitive evidence could be used against the Invisible Boy if it fell into the wrong hands.

I fish a pen out of my backpack and rip the paper in half. The half with his request, I stick in my notepad. I smooth the rest out on the ground and write across the top.

"Can I see you? I have questions."

I fold this over and stick it under the brick. Then I scramble up to Wonder. Last time I was hiding out here, Wonder gave me away—so I need to make sure that doesn't happen again. If I hurry home and back, I can stand watch until the

Invisible Boy shows up. And then I can get an interview for my Junior Journalists contest exposé.

I run back home, Wonder loping at my side. I open the door and unhook her leash, toss it on the front porch, close the door, and rush back to the median. I'm out of breath and sweaty by the time I arrive. I check the bottom of the ditch.

The brick has moved.

I left it white side up. Now it's white side down.

He was here.

Before I've even caught my breath, I'm pulling the brick off and unfolding the torn paper.

Under my question, he's written two lines:

"No one can see me. Please give my picture back."

He must be nearby, since I was only gone for a few minutes. I glance up at the whitewashed house, but the curtains are drawn and everything is still.

No one can see me.

The hairs on my arms stand up. Could he be *here*? Right now? Invisible? I glance around out of the corner of my eye, but of course I can't make out any sign of him. Clearly he doesn't want to meet, but that would never stop Lois Lane, and it won't stop me.

I clear my throat and speak to the air. "Um, hello? I have your picture, and I'd love to hand it to you. So, ah, come on out!"

No response.

Okay. I need another way to lure him into the open.

I pull my notepad out of my backpack and flip to the end, where I've stashed the photo. I pull it free and take a good long look at it. Woman with frizzy hair outside a purple town house, somewhere in DC. The same woman who's in the other picture the Invisible Boy keeps in his hoodie pocket.

I carefully fold some of my own notepad paper around the photo, so it won't get scratched. Then I position it on the ground and lay the brick down white side up.

Once the photo is safe, I casually climb out of the ditch and begin to stroll away from it, in the opposite direction from my house. I go over the cross street and check to see if anyone's around.

No one in sight.

I go down this street's ditch, which is connected to mine by the big concrete pipes. I hunch and enter, hands outstretched on both sides of the tunnel for balance. The first time I met the Invisible Boy, storm water was rushing through here, but now it's almost completely dry. There's just a bit of slime in the very bottom center, and I can waddle through at a crouch without getting my mermaid-scale leggings dirty.

I slip under the street but stop at the other end, while I'm still in the shadows. From here, I can see the brick clearly, but no one will be able to see me until they're already in the ditch.

The perfect spot.

I can't really sit down (because: slime) but I also can't stand up straight. My legs start getting tired. Maybe I could have found a more comfortable place. After all, who knows how long—

A boy in a green T-shirt skids down into the ditch. I catapult from the pipe and run.

My legs are cramped and clumsy. But even so, the boy doesn't notice me—he's nudging the brick over. I dive and tackle him to the ground.

"Ah!" he shrieks.

"I've got you!"

I lean back, victorious—and then reel away in disgust.

I haven't caught the Invisible Boy. Instead, the kid staring up at me is Paddle Boy.

"You!" I gasp. "What are you doing here?"

Paddle Boy sits up. "*Me?* Where did you even come from? You could have cracked my head open!"

"I asked you first!" I point a finger in his face. "Answers. Now."

He glares. "I saw you messing around down here and wanted to know what you were doing."

"This is none of your business." I turn back to the brick. The photo is still there, so I pick it up and tuck it into the safety of my notepad.

"Well you didn't need to try to kill me over it. Jeez, Nadia." He brushes the dirt out of his hair. "What is *wrong* with you?"

My nostrils flare but I just say, "There's nothing wrong with me," and turn on my heel.

Under his breath, he mutters, "That's not what the commenters say."

My muscles tighten. My veins are wired by electricity and lava. I turn slowly. "*Excuse* me?"

He pushes himself to his feet and brushes off his shorts. "You know, my mom wanted to send over more snacks for your family. She still wants your mom to tell her whatever the big secret is before it's announced. But I told her I wouldn't go near your house for anything."

I lift my chin. "Just as well—I only have one paddle left for you to smash."

"Yeah, harp on that some more." He folds his arms over his chest. I'm a little taller than him, but he moves a step up the ditch so he's got a few inches on me. "Do you really have no idea about the big announcement? Don't you call yourself a reporter or something?"

"So what?" I put my notepad and the photo in my backpack, just in case he tries to grab for them.

"If you were any good, wouldn't you know what your own mom is hyping up all over the internet?"

My words come out in a hiss. "I don't care about my mom's blog."

"But this is something about your *family*." He shrugs, lifting that one infuriating eyebrow. "I'd just think you would have figured it out by now. Funny that the whole world's going to hear about it before you do."

My face flames. "You don't know anything!"

"Sure." He rolls his eyes and pushes past me, toward his house. "Do us all a favor—if you're going to crawl around in the sewage, take a bath."

"I wasn't crawling in the sewage!" I yell at his back. "That's just rainwater!"

Over his shoulder, he shouts, "Well, either way, you stink!"

I want to pinch him, or kick his shin, or smash a paddle on his face. Instead, I hitch my backpack up on my shoulders and march with as much dignity as I can to my house. Evidently, today I won't be seeing the Invisible Boy. But it appears I've got another scoop closer to home.

Mom's blog is pretty cool in a lot of ways, I guess—she helps military spouses and she gets enough money from promoting sponsors that she can work from home. I didn't really care about it until last year, when she wrote the now-infamous article, "10 Tips for Raising Tweens in a Military Family." Which included an entire paragraph about how *certain* tweens have a hard time keeping friends, with all the moves, and instead those *special* tweens start obsessing over something odd (like, for instance, comic books), which could make friendships harder . . . It went on from there.

Basically, it was a nightmare.

Almost one thousand words in that entry, all analyzing me. The comments flooded in with suggestions and critiques, and a few weirdos even got into a fight about girls "being brainwashed by the patriarchal narrative" and also whether girls "actually like comics" or just pretend to get boys' attention. Then some moms at school showed it to their kids and those kids showed it to their friends. I got called "blog girl" for a month, a nickname that required so little effort it was almost more insulting because it was so lazy.

Ever since then, we have an unspoken understanding: Mom doesn't directly reference me in her articles (though she can use me for "inspiration"), and I pretend like her blog doesn't exist.

Which apparently means I've missed out on some sort of impending news.

I come into the house and pause to take a deep breath of cool air-conditioned air. It rushes over me like an ice blanket, and some of the heat from my conversation with Paddle Boy seeps away.

Mom calls from upstairs, "That you, Dia?"

"Yes." Wonder Dog dances around me, and I give her a pat as I trudge up toward Mom's voice. There is *not* something wrong with me, no matter what Paddle Boy or random internet people might think. I *am* a good journalist. And I'll get the story before it goes public.

I reach the top of the stairs just in time to see Mom closing the guest bedroom door. She has her hair up in a messy bun and is wearing paint-splattered jeans and a T-shirt.

She smiles. "I thought you came home when Wonder showed up, but then I couldn't find you. Off hunting a story?"

"It didn't really work out." I shrug, then lean to look around her at the closed door. "What are you doing?"

"Oh—I wanted to talk to you about that!" Mom grins, rubbing her hands with a washcloth. "I decided to start doing podcasts! The room up here will have perfect acoustics for a studio, I think. But while I'm renovating, it's off-limits. I want the final product to be a big surprise."

She rocks a little on her feet, excited. I try to look excited, too, but I almost can't believe it was that easy. A podcast studio? That's the big announcement? I guess she *has* been talking about this for a long time, but I doubt anyone besides her biggest fans will be as pumped about it as she is. A harder investigation would have been more fun to rub in Paddle Boy's face. I can't really even call this an investigation, it was so easy.

Too easy?

"Man, I'm hungry." Mom checks the time on her phone. "What do you say to a little midafternoon popcorn and iced tea?"

"Sounds good. I'm just going to—um—put my stuff in my room." I head down the hall.

"See you in a sec, then." Mom goes back downstairs.

I wait in my doorway until she's out of sight, and a little longer until I hear the microwave start. Then I sneak back to the guest bedroom door. Even if it is just a new office, I could still get the scoop before the rest of the world. Snap a few pictures. And that would prove that I'm a good journalist. And show Paddle Boy he is wrong.

I put my hand on the cold doorknob and give it a turn.

It doesn't move.

Frowning, I try again. It's locked.

I bend down for a better look. The doors in our house lock from the inside, but even though this doorknob looks the same as the rest—a silver handle—I can instantly tell that Mom's replaced it. Because this doorknob has a keyhole on the outside.

Why would she think a studio needed a special lock? I get that she's excited about her new space, but this is a bit much.

Too much?

From downstairs, Mom calls, "Nadia! Popcorn's ready!"

I give the door one last frown, then head to the living room. Mom has set out two bowls of popcorn and two tall glasses of iced tea. She's scrolling on her phone and doesn't look up until I've sat down, cross-legged, with my bowl in my lap.

"I was really interested to meet James and his grandmother

at the party," Mom tells me, putting aside her phone. "It's so odd that we didn't know Mrs. B better before this. She's lived in that house for nearly twenty years." She eats a piece of popcorn. "But I guess that's Northern Virginia for you—no one is out of doors long enough to get to know their neighbors."

"Or if they are out of doors, they're smashing your stuff," I mutter.

Mom gives me a smile. "Have you ever *asked* Kenny why he smashed the paddle?"

"Mom. His name is Paddle Boy."

"Okay, okay." Mom shrugs a little. "Just seems like there might be a story worth telling there."

I grimace. "He's evil. There's nothing to uncover."

"Anyway. Did you know Mrs. B's late husband was retired navy?"

I shake my head. "I just knew he died of cancer."

"Apparently he was injured in a car accident on his way to work, and while he was in recovery he got diagnosed with lung cancer. Never smoked a day in his life, Mrs. B says. But even while he was in chemo, Veterans Affairs refused to compensate him for his injuries. I think there's a story here that my audience will appreciate."

Mom does a lot of different sorts of content—Do-It-Yourself guides, recipes, 20-things-you-didn't-know-about-whatever—but these feature stories are not terrible. Sometimes I even read them. They're the closest she gets to being kind of like a reporter. "Are you going to do an interview with Mrs. B?"

Mom nods. "Yes, I think so. Maybe in a few days—I need to check what her schedule is like."

An idea begins to form in my mind. "Do you think you could do it at Riverside Park?"

Mom blinks. "What?"

"If you do it there, it'd be like—atmospheric. With birds and stuff." The park is on the bike trail my parents and I use on weekends, and it's only about a five-minute walk from our house. "And also James is doing photography of wildlife around here, and I think there's an eagle nest near the park. So he could come, too."

Mom nods slowly. "Not that I have anything against the man, but why do I need James Wilson to be present . . . ?"

I shrug casually. Just because he blew it at Little Hunting Jr., and at the house party, doesn't mean I can't give the poor guy another shot. "Because maybe Aunt Lexie and I could go on a bike ride that day."

"*Aha.*" Mom taps the side of her nose. "Well, I think that could certainly be arranged."

I smile and throw a handful of my popcorn into my mouth. Paddle Boy might be onto the secret studio story (though it is *suspiciously* secret for something so boring), but one thing's for sure: No one *makes* stories happen like Nadia Quick.

Chapter 7

GIRL REPORTER SAVES DAY, NOT DATE

Aunt Lexie suspects nothing.

We started out on the ride Friday afternoon. She borrowed my mom's bike, and I'm on my own with Wonder Dog attached via her dog-friendly biking leash. My family regularly goes on rides along the Mount Vernon Trail, sometimes to Old Town Alexandria, and sometimes we even veer off to visit Washington, DC. Today, Aunt Lexie and I go about a mile and then turn back around to return to Riverside Park.

"I know I said I want to exercise more," Aunt Lexie pants, coming up beside me on the trail, "but maybe I should wait until winter!"

I snicker. This heat is wimpy. Clouds gather on the horizon, dark blue and gray and angry. More thunderstorms tonight, probably. But none of this is anywhere close to the weather down in the real South.

"Is your mom still doing this?" Aunt Lexie asks. "Biking—and stuff?"

"Yeah, sure." I shrug. "We did a short route last week."

Aunt Lexie frowns. "Hmm."

I glance over at her. Her face is red and shiny. "Why?"

She slows to fall behind me as we approach some walkers. "No reason."

We come around a bend and clatter over a wooden bridge. Ahead, I spot Mom sitting at a picnic table with Mrs. B. James Wilson is nowhere in sight right now, but Mom promised she'd find a way to bring him along. Maybe he's off taking pictures—which would be great, because then I could get Aunt Lexie to wash her face first. Meeting up with him *after* biking might not have been one of my more brilliant ideas.

We cruise into the park. Once I leave the smooth paved trail, the ground bounces and my bike bucks under me. Wonder Dog gives an excited bark as I pull to a stop.

"Hey there, Dia," Mom says with a smile and a wink. "Hi, Lex."

I hop off and switch Wonder onto a normal leash before she can pull my bike over. Aunt Lexie takes off her helmet and wipes her forehead with a corner of her shirt.

"Good afternoon, Mrs. B," she says. "What are you two doing?"

"Interview." Mom holds up her phone, which has the recording app active. "Mrs. B was just telling me about her husband's experience with veterans affairs."

Mrs. B nods. "It's a beautiful day to be out. Seemed a shame to spend it cooped up."

"At least indoors has air-conditioning," Aunt Lexie says with a laugh. "Nadia's been putting me through biking boot camp. I could barely keep up!"

Over Aunt Lexie's shoulder, I spot James. He's coming from a path in the woods, his camera in hand and his head angled up while he looks at the trees. I dig in my backpack and pass Lexie a bottle of water and my hand towel, just as a gentle hint. She takes a long drink, then pours a bit on the towel and wipes her face. It's not a whole lot of improvement, but it's something.

"Hi, Lexie." James approaches, wearing the same goofy smile that appeared when he was around Aunt Lexie at the party. "Hey, Nadia. I didn't know you were here."

"Hi, James." I move back a little to nudge Aunt Lexie

toward him. "Me and my aunt were on the trail. We did five miles, round trip."

"Wow, in this heat?" James glances at Aunt Lexie and smiles.

"Nadia's exaggerating a bit," she says, smiling back. Then she turns to Mrs. B. "Is it okay if I join you? I think my legs are turning to jelly."

"Why don't we go sit over there?" I blurt, pointing to a perfectly romantic bench nearer the water.

"I think your aunt might want to get out of the sun," Mrs. B offers in a good-humored tone. Belatedly, I realize that my selection is in full sunlight, while this place is in shade. Mrs. B pats the bench next to her. "Come on and rest your bones a bit."

"Are you sure?" Mom asks Mrs. B, though she glances in my direction. "I know sometimes it can be awkward to do an interview in front of someone else . . ."

"Oh, that's no problem." Mrs. B waves away Mom's concern. Aunt Lexie sinks down with a grateful thanks and sips from the bottle.

Me, James, and Wonder Dog stand off to the side. Mom shrugs at me. This is not going the way I'd hoped.

Then things get even worse.

"Hey, Nadia," says the most irritating voice in the universe, somehow directly behind me.

I whirl and narrow my eyes. Paddle Boy.

"What are you doing here?" I demand. Does he know I still have the Invisible Boy's picture in my backpack? Does he hope to send me and my dog to the depths of the Potomac?

"Waiting for my dad." Paddle Boy shifts his backpack higher up on his shoulders. "What about you? You look hot—" His face goes red. "Warm. Because it's hot outside."

"I went biking." I glance at James, but he's walked off, carrying an empty bottle to the water fountain. I kneel down and loop Wonder's leash around the picnic-table leg so she can crawl under to lie in the shade. Paddle Boy's mom has always seemed semi-normal, but I've never met his dad. Maybe that's where the supervillain influence comes from. "Are you like . . . going to have a family picnic or something?"

"Erm. No." Paddle Boy points to the parking lot, where a car is stopped with the engine still on. His mom is texting in the driver's seat. "I'm spending the weekend with him in Arlington. My mom doesn't really like to have him by the house, so we meet here."

A new hope fills my chest. "So you'll be gone the entire weekend?"

"Don't sound too excited." He kind of smiles.

A weekend isn't a whole lot of time to be free of him, but I will take what I can get. Though I should keep an eye on news in Arlington. Make sure he's not up to too much trouble there.

Casually, I ask, "Where in Arlington does your dad live?"

"Near Iwo Jima Memorial. I can see it from my window." He shrugs, then hesitates before pulling out a sheet from his backpack. Gel window stickers. "Um."

My jaw drops.

Superman stickers.

"For my new room," Paddle Boy says. "At my dad's place."

I can't help staring. "You like . . . Superman?"

"Yeah. I haven't read the comics, but I've seen almost all of the animated series." He shrugs again and puts the stickers back in his bag. "Your mom said you like him?"

Any momentary curiosity drains right back out of me. He would have found that out from Mom's blog. I know she's done at least one entry about "How to Encourage Military Kids' Interests," where she talked for a long time about how she "fostered" my "obsession" with Superman. (Never mind that Aunt Lexie's the one who introduced me to the cartoons, and Dad bought my first comic book, and I am most interested in Lois Lane, which isn't the same thing as being all about Superman.)

"I like Lois Lane," I answer, flat-toned.

I take my bike and turn to Mom. She's scribbling notes while Mrs. B talks and Aunt Lexie listens in perplexed indignation (the usual reaction for anything related to Veterans Affairs). James returns and passes Aunt Lexie the newly filled water bottle. She mumbles, "Thanks, Nadia," without looking away from Mrs. B.

When there's a pause, I clear my throat. "Mom, can I head home?"

Aunt Lexie blinks at me in surprise. I subtly point at James so she'll realize he got her the water.

Mom glances over. "Not by yourself."

"It's not that far," I complain, embarrassed that she's treating me like a kid in front of Paddle Boy.

Mom shakes her head. "We drove here—why don't you go ahead and hook your bike to the car?"

I blow a strand of hair out of my face, lift my chin, and march past Paddle Boy to the parking lot. He follows me after a minute, like a mosquito buzzing around my head. I ignore him as I lift my bike and strap it on the carrier.

Paddle Boy kicks a pine cone with his shoe. It rolls to a stop against my foot. "Look, Nadia. It's not *my* fault that your mom talks about you on the blog."

"Yeah, but *you* read it," I hiss over my shoulder.

"If you don't want her to write about you, why don't you just tell her to take down those old entries?"

Honestly. A journalist wouldn't impose on someone else's freedom of speech—even if that freedom led to said journalist's eternal mortification. It's easier to just pretend I'll never have to interact with people who read about me. The kids at school have mostly forgotten "blog girl" and moved on. Though, obviously, Paddle Boy persists in bringing it up. So maybe other kids from school still remember Mom's entries.

I decide it's time to change the subject. I turn to face him, hands on hips. "I figured out my mom's big announcement."

"Oh." He blinks. "Cool?"

"She's starting a podcast," I tell him. It sounds even more lame out loud. Lame, and anticlimactic. But if that's the story she's trying to sell, I might as well sell it, too.

One eyebrow lifts. "That's it?"

Inwardly, I completely agree. But I can't let him know that. "She's making a whole studio. It's going to be very neat when she finishes and reveals everything. She's letting me help put it together."

"Okay." He looks pretty bored now.

"So I am a good journalist," I clarify, trying to make my point. I kick the pine cone hard, and it bounces off his ankle.

"Okay," he says again, frowning and kicking it back.

I roll my eyes. "Have a great weekend, Paddle Boy."

"Kenny," he corrects. "How would you like it if I called you Journalist Girl?"

"I would be absolutely fine with that, Kevin." I flip one of my two braids over my shoulder, give the pine cone a final kick in his direction, and head back to Mom and the others.

Something light and prickly bounces off my back. He says, "Kenny."

I turn around. The pine cone we'd been kicking is on the ground. He threw it at me! I pick it up and toss it at him, not really aiming to hit him, just annoyed. "Quit it, Kirk."

He catches the pine cone. He tosses it in one hand, up and down. "Bet you can't get this back."

"Why would I want to, Kennedy?"

His eyes sharpen. "Because if you do, I'll tell you something about that boy—the one you keep looking for."

I stare at him, not breathing for a second. Then, before I

can think better of it, I dive at him. Paddle Boy bounds back. He's grinning, like we're playing some sort of game. I focus on just getting the stupid pine cone back. If he has information about the Invisible Boy, then there's no way I'm giving up. Paddle Boy runs around parked cars, using the lot like a maze.

"Stop being dumb!" I call after him. "Watch where you're going!"

"Hey, check this." He tilts his face up and puts the pine cone on his nose. It balances there for a second.

I jump forward to grab it, but he jerks away with a laugh. The pine cone falls.

In the corner of my eye, I see red.

A car. Speeding through the parking lot.

I grab Paddle Boy out of the middle of the lane and yank him toward me. We both fall against another car and land in a heap.

The red car screeches to a stop. I've landed half under Paddle Boy. My chest has frozen—I can't get any air.

"Nadia?!" Paddle Boy gasps, jumping off me.

I can't answer. My chest won't move.

Out of nowhere, Mom grabs me and pulls me into a hug. All at once, breath whooshes into my lungs. I cough and gasp.

"Oh my gosh! Are you okay?" Mom asks, leaning back so she can get a look at me. "Did you hit your head?"

I blink. My elbow stings—it's scraped and bleeding. My chest feels bruised. "I don't think so."

Aunt Lexie wraps her arm around my shoulder. "That was amazing, Nadia! You reacted so quickly!"

James and Mrs. B are there, too, and other adults who saw what happened. They pepper me with questions and compliments and concerns. Some of them argue with the driver. On the other side of the small crowd, there's Paddle Boy and his mom. My gaze catches on the pine cone, right where we stood. It's flattened. In pieces.

I hear Paddle Boy's mom say, "How could you be so thoughtless, Kenny? You could have gotten hurt!"

He mumbles a reply I can't make out. A twinge of something strange and sour sinks into my stomach.

I look around at the faces, all concerned and proud and talking. Paddle Boy and I could've been run over.

And the Invisible Boy didn't come.

Maybe it's because Paddle Boy was involved. And Paddle Boy is a supervillain, and heroes aren't obligated to save supervillains—right?

I look up as Paddle Boy and his mom walk over to me. His head is bowed.

"Thanks, Nadia," he says. "Sorry I . . . Yeah."

"It's okay," I blurt, not sure how else I'm supposed to

respond. This time, I know he didn't orchestrate it. He's the one who almost got hit.

"Look," he adds, lowering his voice and leaning toward me so his mom can't hear. "That boy. I've seen him out in front of the house on the corner. Twice. At night. Super late. Doing something with the lawn. He never left the yard."

"Oh." That's not a lot of information. But my head rings and I can't think straight.

Paddle Boy's mom keeps a hand tight on his shoulder and marches him to their car. He doesn't look too much like a supervillain right now.

Heroes save people, no matter who they are. Even I, the archenemy of Paddle Boy, saved his life just now. That can't be the reason the Invisible Boy didn't rescue us.

So . . .

Superman has super speed—and he can fly—which makes protecting people pretty easy. But maybe the Invisible Boy doesn't. Maybe the Invisible Boy has a limited range. Like, he can only sense danger that's closer to his home base. He's only ever showed up on my street before.

An idea blooms in my head.

I know how to catch—or rather, be caught by—a hero.

Chapter 8

HOW TO CATCH A SUPERHERO

You going out already?" Mom asks.

We just got home, and I let Wonder have a drink before I went right back to the door. Now Aunt Lexie and Mom are looking at me like I've lost my mind.

"I have to test something," I explain without explaining. "It won't take too long!"

Before they can protest, I rush off to put my plan into action. Wonder Dog doesn't seem to mind the extra walk. We circle the street twice to find the perfect location for my experiment: right across from the Invisible Boy's house. Perfect.

I loop Wonder's leash around a tree trunk and toss my backpack down beside her. Pin prickles race up and down my neck. I'm being watched. I don't even bother to look—I won't be able to see the Invisible Boy.

I reach up and swing my legs to hook them around the lowest branch. I maneuver to the top of the limb and reach for the next one.

When I'm about twelve, maybe fifteen feet off the ground, I test my grip and edge away from the trunk, sloth-style. Blood heats my head, but I keep going until the branch starts to bend. With a quick glance, I check the ground below. I'm over the paved street, just a few other branches between me and a nasty fall.

Excellent.

When I call out, the warble of excitement sounds convincingly like a panicked kid. "HELP! HELP! I'M STUCK!"

Wonder gives a few worried barks. Good. That will draw attention.

"I'm stuck and I can't get down!" I wail in my most desperate voice. "I might just fall!"

The neighborhood, however, gives no response. Everything is quiet. Abandoned.

Blowing a strand of hair out of my face, I try to shift my aching hands. But when I settle them into a new spot, something buzzes against my palm.

Bee!

I jerk without thinking, lose my hold entirely, and plummet with a scream. I claw air for a second, then my arm smacks into one of the lower branches. I cling to it, legs waving over emptiness.

Wonder yowls, frantic, and I can't think over the sound of her barks and the humming in my head. The wood creaks. The branch bends under my weight. *Oh no.* It holds for a breath, and I don't dare blink.

Then it snaps.

I fall. Before my life can flash before my eyes or I can get air to scream again, I hit the ground with a heavy thud.

Except. I'm not on hot asphalt.

"Ouch," groans a voice below me.

I landed on someone.

I'm sitting on someone's chest.

The Invisible Boy, wearing the red hoodie and fully visible, rubs his face as he winces up at me.

I can't help it. I let out a loud whoop and fist-pump the sky. "I found you!"

"Can you—um—move?" he asks hoarsely. "I can't exactly—"

"Oh yes, sure! Right!" I scramble to stand up, beaming at him. To my yappy dog, I murmur, "Shush."

The boy pushes himself up carefully. He looks pretty much the same as I remember—his skin a shade lighter than mine, his hair somewhere between brown and black. It's straight and hacked, like it was cut with kiddie scissors. His jeans are faded and raggedy at the hem and around the knees. He's barefoot. I'd guess he's a year or two older than me. Maybe fourteen.

"Oh my gosh," I gasp. "It worked. I can't believe it *worked*!"

The Invisible Boy frowns at me, but then in one quick movement he rolls over, gets his feet beneath him, and bolts.

"No!" I shriek, tackling his legs and sending him sprawling before he can vanish. "You're not going anywhere until I get answers!"

He wiggles around so he can face me. His dark eyes could shoot laser beams if he had heat vision, so I guess it's a good thing he apparently doesn't.

"No way are you just disappearing again," I declare, keeping ahold of his ankles. "I want an interview!"

"A—what?" He looks from me to Wonder, who's still barking her head off.

"Where do you live?" I ask. Like an ace reporter, I launch my questions rapid-fire. "What's your name? Why weren't you there when Paddle Boy almost got run over? Where did you come from? Mars? Krypton?" I narrow my eyes. "Texas?"

"Can you let me go?" he says. He tries to kick me off. "I need to get back inside."

"Why? What's inside? What are you working on?"

The Invisible Boy struggles, trying to yank his legs free. "Who *are* you?"

"A journalist." I grin. "And I want the exclusive on whatever scoop you're dishing."

"What does that—?" The boy's eyes dart toward Wonder Dog—still barking—and the other houses. "Can you—?"

"Look, I'll sweeten the deal. I won't tell anyone where you live. You live in that house right there, yeah? The white one?"

He just stares at me without answering. I press on.

"I'll interview you there, so you don't even have to leave. I won't get in your way. I just want to see what you do. But you have to promise not to disappear on me again!"

I hold my breath while he thinks. He could just turn invisible right now, right in front of me, and—disintegrate into the air. I won't be able to find him if he hides. He could drop off my radar; it wouldn't be hard.

"Monday," he says suddenly. "One thirty."

That would leave me hanging—metaphorically—for two whole days. "Can't I come sooner?"

"No. Not on weekends. Monday, or nothing."

"Fine. I'll be there." I lift my hands off his ankles.

Immediately, he springs to his feet and takes off toward

the whitewashed house. At the last moment, he veers for the gate to the backyard.

I call after him, "Hey!"

The Invisible Boy skids to a stop and looks back.

I lift my hand in a wave. "Thanks for saving my life!"

He blinks. A smile appears—a wide, sudden smile. Then he ducks through the gate.

———— //////////// ————

Monday. 1:25. Wonder Dog and I—having narrowly survived a weekend of suspense—approach the gate. I have a sense he's not going to open the front door, and I saw him run in here last time, so it seems likely that he might be waiting in the backyard.

In front of the fence, I take a deep breath and savor the moment. A few small steps for girl and dog, one giant leap for reporting-kind. Today, I'm getting a real interview with a real superhero.

I pull my Lois Lane press pass from under my shirt and fix it across my chest. Straightening my shoulders, I lift my hand to knock.

Before my hand falls, the Invisible Boy pulls open the gate, looking at me like I've broken the law. "You're early."

"Hi!" I grin. "How are you today?"

"Shh." He glances over my shoulder at Mrs. B's empty yard. Reluctantly, he makes room for me to pass through the gate, closing it swiftly behind me. "Keep your voice down."

Wonder Dog pulls the leash and has a sniff at the Invisible Boy's bare feet. He holds still for a moment, then offers her his hand. She gives it a sniff and nuzzles her face against his fingers.

"She likes you," I point out.

A smile pulls at his mouth, but he seems to swallow it down. "What's her name?"

"Wonder Dog. Can I let her off the leash? Your fence goes all the way around, right?"

He hesitates. "Will she dig?"

I huff. "She is a civilized dog. She will not dig."

He nods slowly. I unhook her leash and Wonder goes off sniffing. For the first time, I really examine the yard. At night, it looked pretty. But it's a thousand times more beautiful in the daylight. It's like the centerfold in my grandma's *Home & Garden* magazine. Flowers spring up in well-ordered bunches, little mulch paths meander into a maze of color, the firepit is spotlessly clean and surrounded by matching outdoor chairs, arranged in the perfect reading spots.

"Uh, so there is one rule if you're going to talk to me," the Invisible Boy says, shifting on his feet. "You have to promise to tell no one about me. Or this. Or anything."

I already promised not to tell anyone where he lived, but this sounds like standard superhero protocol. I nod. I can always get his approval for my article later, when he's ready for me to take it public. "Okay. I promise."

"Right. Good."

"Oh! And"—I pull the picture of his mom out of my notepad—"here you go. I kept it safe."

"Thank you." He takes the photo carefully and studies it a moment, a solemn expression in his eyes. Then he tucks it into his hoodie pocket and zips it closed. He pauses. "You said you had questions?"

I look him up and down. Even with my bribe/gift, he's more tense than a jack-in-the-box ready to spring. If I ask him for the real scoop right now, he'll outright deny the truth—or try to get me to leave. I need him to trust me before I can count on him being honest.

So I smile in my best harmless-girl way. "I don't think we've been properly introduced." I hold out my hand. "I'm Nadia Quick."

He pauses. Small circular scars on his arm shimmer when he shakes with me. "Eli."

His skin is coated in a layer of dirt. I glance behind him at some of the flower beds. "Were you gardening?"

"Um, yes. And—I can't talk long. I need to get a lot done today."

"I can help," I volunteer. One way to get people comfortable around you is to share their interests. Every good reporter knows that. "I do gardening sometimes with my grandparents."

He hesitates again. If I didn't know better, I'd think he's just a timid preteen boy who doesn't do anything without heaps of anxiety. But of course, that is the perfect alternate identity for a superhero. It's almost the same as Clark Kent's act. No one would suspect this boy is capable of jumping into a rushing river or catching someone midair.

"I—suppose you can help." He walks toward one of the mulch paths. A pile of smooth stones sits at the edge of the patio. "I was finishing off the trail edging," he explains. "Some weeds have grown up around the rocks, so I had to pull them and . . . yeah. I'm just putting these back now."

I pick up one of the rocks, prepared to get an armful, but they're heavier than I expected. The Invisible Boy—Eli—casually loads at least six into his arms. Super strength might need to be added to his list of powers. I manage to add another rock to my own haul, but there's no way I can carry more without dropping them.

Eli heads down the path, his bare feet making absolutely no noise on the mulch. I crunch along behind him.

"Do you like superheroes?" I blurt.

"I . . . what?" He glances at me, confused.

"Superheroes. You know." Wonder Dog trots on my heels, and I nudge her away a little. Even with just these two rocks, my arms are getting tired fast. "DC Comics. Marvel. Do you have a favorite superhero?"

Eli doesn't answer. He gets to the end of the stone-edged path and kneels, carefully putting down his pile. I add my rocks next to his, then watch while he carefully examines one, finds the apparently superior side to put faceup, and places it exactly at the edge of the mulch. I start wondering if he's ever going to answer.

"I like Spider-Man," he says at last. "And Batman."

"They're cool!" I exclaim, so excited that he actually replied that I forget to keep my voice down.

He glances in the direction of Mrs. B's house, and I quickly whisper, "Sorry."

"Do . . . you have a favorite?" he asks.

"Superman." I kneel opposite Eli and put the next stone

down. Wonder Dog flops on her side in a circle of sunlight, apparently ready for a nap. "Superman is the best, in my opinion."

"Isn't he kind of . . . boring?" Eli takes the stone I just placed and nudges it a little closer to the mulch, adjusting its angle so it makes a clean link to the one before it. "He's practically invincible."

I shake my head. "No, it isn't about how he has all these amazing powers—though that's really neat. What's great about Superman is that he's got all of that, but he has to *hide* it. He has to be a normal person when really he's a billion times stronger and faster and more incredible than regular people. It's not about how Superman *can* level a city without even trying, it's about how he has to *try not to*."

I stop to catch my breath. Eli is watching me—well, watching in a general-direction sort of way. Not actually looking me in the face. This is when most kids at school—or anonymous commenters—would tell me I'm weird or wrong or something. But Eli's listening. Excitement makes my pulse race.

"And that's what is so freakin' cool about him and Lois Lane," I gush. "Lois Lane is an ace reporter, but she's also just a plain old human being. And whatever people say, she *is* crazy smart."

"I thought she never realized Superman was Clark Kent

because of his glasses." Eli makes circles with his fingers and holds them over his eyes. "How would anyone be fooled by that?"

I shoot him my most serious glare. "Okay, mister. If your teacher looked exactly like the president of the United States, would you assume it actually *was* the president? And just, like, hanging around your school for the fun of it? Or would you think they're two different people?"

"Oh."

"That's right." I nod, pleased. "You have to remember, Superman's been around since like the 1940s—tons of different people have written his comics. Sometimes they make the characters act really dumb. But there are so many good stories, too! I could bring my favorites to show you. I'll have you converted in no time. Anyway—" Time to start circling to my real questions. I put another rock down, which Eli almost immediately repositions. "What's your favorite superpower?"

"Flying," he says, almost immediately.

Not what I expected. I'm almost disappointed.

But clearly I've just asked the wrong question. I asked for *favorite*, not *actual*. Maybe flying isn't one of his actual superpowers, and he'd *like* to have that one. Doesn't mean he can't turn invisible.

"I'd like to stop time," I tell him, "so I can always record my observations." I glance over at Wonder Dog, sprawled out in her sunshine spot. "I think Wonder would like super speed so she can catch human food before it even touches the ground." He doesn't say anything to that, still busy with the rocks. I've given up on helping, because every time I put one down, he fixes it. "Okay, so, what would your name be?"

"Huh?" He glances toward me.

"Your superhero name." I pause, letting him mull it over. "Perhaps . . . the Invisible Boy?"

He frowns. "I . . . suppose. Why would a flying superhero be called that?"

"Because if you're going to fly around this area, you definitely need to have some camouflage." I grin at him. "I think when I stop time, it looks like I flash from one place to the next—just, BAM, I'm somewhere else. So, I'll be Lightning Lane."

"Lane—like the reporter?" he asks.

I nod. "Right—like, a superhero but still in the Lane family. Like the superhero sister. Who's also a reporter."

"Oh." He doesn't look any less confused, but he pushes himself to his feet and brushes dirt off his knees. "I need to get more stones."

"Aye, aye." I hop up and follow him. "How many can you carry at once?"

He frowns, thinking. Most boys I know (cough Paddle Boy cough) would say something dumb and exaggerated just to seem extra cool, but Eli takes the question seriously. "I did ten once," he says slowly. "But the hardest part is keeping them all balanced while I hold them. If someone else helped, I could probably do more."

"Want me to stack them on you and see?" I ask, curious myself. For scientific research.

"Sure." His eyes brighten. When we get to the pile, he cradles his arms in front of him. One by one, I place the rocks, being extra careful to ensure each one is secure.

"Tell me when it gets too heavy," I remind him, once we've passed eleven stones. He's so wiry and skinny; I'm more impressed than ever that he doesn't just buckle under this weight.

Eli doesn't speak for another three stones. Then he nods and tucks his chin over the highest one to hold it. "I think that's enough."

"Okay." I grab just one for myself. "I'm right here if you need me to take some."

Stoically, Eli turns and makes his way down the path again. I watch, but he seems totally fine—he doesn't even wobble when he sets them down in our new spot. Maybe this isn't a case of a superstrength superhero (who, I imagine, would take on more like fifty stones), but it is still supercool.

"That's awesome," I blurt. "How did you get so good at this?"

He shrugs. "Practice?"

I make a mental note to add to my record later, and move on to my next question. After the incident with Paddle Boy in the parking lot, I want to find a way to be sure Eli will come save the day if he's needed. "So, if you were Batman, what would you use instead of a Bat-Signal? Like, how would someone let you know they needed help?"

Eli leans back on his heels. "Would it need to be a symbol in the sky?"

I shake my head. "Not necessarily. Just something you'd be able to notice from a distance."

While Eli is thinking, his stomach lets loose a huge rumble. Like, I can hear it standing next to him. I feel my cheeks get hot, but he doesn't even seem to notice. I wonder how long he's been working out here.

"Maybe we should take a break?" I suggest. "For, like, a snack or something?"

"No, I need to finish this up." Eli presses a hand to his middle, then leans forward to continue placing rocks. "If I was a superhero, I would use a mourning-dove call."

"A what?"

He searches the treetops around us and points to a pigeon-like bird with pretty brown feathers. "That's a mourning dove. They have a really distinct song." He cups his hands around his mouth and makes a funny birdlike sound, sort of like, *Woo WOO ooo ooo ooo*. The bird in the tree swivels its head, cocking it one way and then the other in confusion.

I giggle and try to mimic the call. "Woo OOO ooo woo."

The bird flies away. Eli grins—that nice grin that just appears all of a sudden. "Softer than that." He demonstrates again.

I plant my hands on my hips. "That sounds exactly like what I just did!"

"Yours sounds more like a person," he says. "Mourning doves do it really gently. Sort of floating."

I smile. "You're going to have to come up with an easier signal if you want anyone to get ahold of you. And anyway—if it sounds just like a bird, how will you know whether it's that dove or a person needing help?"

"I'd use my super hearing to tell the difference," he says offhandedly, working on the next stone.

"Do you have that?" I ask, a bit too eagerly.

Eli frowns and then lifts his eyebrows. "Um. No."

"Just wondering." I shrug and study the trees around us like they're the most interesting things I've ever seen. Before

I can come up with another angle to try to get him to talk about his real secret identity, my phone buzzes in my pocket. I dig it out and a text from Mom flashes on the screen.

Mom 2:12 p.m.

> You've been gone on your walk for a while! Did you get lost? ;)

The winky face means she's sort of joking. But it has been a while. If I leave now, I can claim Wonder Dog and I just went on a longer-than-usual stroll. I promised Eli I wouldn't tell anyone about him, and a good reporter keeps her sources confidential. So I need to act like everything's normal.

"My mom wants me at home." I turn to Eli. "Can I come tomorrow?"

He freezes, halfway to putting down another rock. "I . . ."

"I'll help with the gardening again! Look how fast we got stuff done today." Never mind that he did most of it and I just stacked rocks. I press on, giving him a thumbs-up with one hand while I grab Wonder's leash and hook it on with my other. "It'll be great. Okay? I'll come at one thirty. See you then!"

Before he can protest, Wonder and I are out the gate.

Chapter 9

THE CARING AND KEEPING OF VETERANS

When I get back home from an early walk on Tuesday morning, Mom's not in her office, even though she was working on some important blog entry when I left. I take off Wonder Dog's leash.

"Mom?" I call, scratching at my itchy elbow. The new scab from saving Paddle Boy pinches my skin whenever I bend my arm.

"Here!"

I lean over the stairs to look up and spot Mom leaving the ex-guest-room/new-studio-in-progress. She shuts the door before I can see more than pastel-pink walls. Weird choice of color.

"How is it outside?" she asks, coming down with a bounce to her step. "I'm thinking about going to Old Town to have a chat with a guy about his military-friendly business. Want to come with?" She slips past me on her way to pull out her biking shoes. "I know it sounds boring, but I suspect it will actually be pretty cool. And we can grab some Nicecream while we're in town."

"Are you going to bike?" I ask, though it's an obvious question. "When Aunt Lexie and I were out, she seemed kind of concerned about that."

"Pfft, Lexie is a worrier." Mom blows a strand of hair off her face, then pauses to redo her ponytail. "You don't have to come along. I know an eight-mile ride isn't exactly what the kids call 'fun' these days, but all this room setup has me stir-crazy!"

"What time do you think we'd be back?" I ask, thinking of my one thirty appointment with Eli.

"Definitely before noon. I don't want to be out during the middle of the day."

Aunt Lexie is *kind* of a worrier, but also when she worries, she tends to be right about things. It'd be better if Mom didn't bike alone, either way. And the offer of Nicecream is too good to pass up. "I'll come. But I think it's too hot for Wonder."

Mom nods. "Why don't you get her settled while I grab the bikes?"

Ten minutes later, Mom and I are turning off Wakefield Street and onto Stratford Lane. We go right past Eli's house, and I sneak a look at the windows. Curtains and stillness, per normal. No one would suspect a superhero lives there.

We bike down to George Washington Parkway, cross over to the Potomac side, and join the paved trail that snakes all the way from Mount Vernon past Washington, DC, to Roosevelt Island. I know, because me and my parents have done the whole route before. All eighteen miles of it.

There's not enough room on the bike lanes for us to stay side by side, so Mom cruises ahead. I hit my regular speed and zone out, watching the woods in their green-gold haze and catching glimpses of the Potomac. The huge river might look pretty under the blue sky today, but it's really a tan-brown color. Every now and then I get a whiff of the smell—salty dead fish. My heartbeat shifts to match the rhythm of my pedaling. Sunlight and shadows race over my hands. Every time I bend or straighten my arms, the scab at my elbow stings.

We stop for a water break about halfway to town, in a shady part of the trail with some benches. I sip at my water and scratch my arm.

Mom swats my hand lightly. "Don't pick that scab."

I didn't even realize I *was* picking it. "Oops."

Mom turns me to get a good look at it and sighs. She splashes some of her water onto a tissue, then wipes off fresh blood. "We'll stop and get you some Band-Aids," she tells me. "If you keep fussing with this, it's not going to heal right."

"We have Band-Aids at home," I remind her, rubbing the now-clean elbow.

"I'm sure we do." Mom moves my hand away again. "But we're getting some on this ride. I want that scrape covered."

I sigh, but there's no arguing with Mom when she gets like this. Soon, we're back on the bikes and heading into town. We stop at the CVS, where Mom grabs more bottles of water and a small first aid kit. She makes me open it outside, drench the scrape in antibiotic ointment, and put on a big Band-Aid that almost immediately starts to wrinkle, apparently not pleased being stretched over the elbow.

Mom nods, though, satisfied. "Okay. On to Synergy, then!"

"On to what?" I ask. The sidewalks are wide and empty here, so I can ride beside her.

"Synergy Float Center," she tells me. "Owned by a veteran. They do lots of alternative treatments for things like

PTSD—it's amazing work. Some of my readers have been asking for a feature about creative ways to help a spouse returning from combat, and I think Chris—that's the owner—I think he'll have interesting ideas."

Float Center. I recognize the words. I think my mom goes there sometimes for migraines? Which would make sense, if that's how she found out about this guy. By the time we reach the office, even I'm feeling a little hot. Not Mississippi-hot, but enough to look forward to air-conditioning.

We chain our bikes up outside. Mom goes right inside, but I pause to check my lock.

Down the street, someone calls, "Girl!"

I jump, surprised.

A man comes around the corner, moving quickly but with a lurch every other step. He has a strange tool in one hand, and with his other he's pushing a cart filled with bags. He has wiry gray-brown hair and is wearing army camouflage.

"Girl!" he calls again. His gaze slides past me and the cars without ever rising higher than my knees. "Girl!"

My muscles tense, and my stomach tightens. I don't think he's talking to me. But what is he up to?

He's coming in my direction. I hurry inside. A cold blast of air hits my face. Peaceful piano music plays in the waiting room, and the air smells pure, with a hint of something flowery. I look over my shoulder and out the large front windows. The man is still wandering around, shouting.

"I'm glad you've had a good ride here, Mrs. Quick," the lady behind the counter is saying to Mom. "Chris told me to watch for you. Let me just go get him."

"Is it okay if I hop in your bathroom first?" Mom asks with a laugh, pushing back her hair.

The lady smiles and points to the door. While Mom goes to freshen up, I find a seat near the window and sip my water.

The man passes the window. He seems to be whispering now, but I can see his mouth moving. "Girl? Girl?"

I lean forward to watch while he goes to the opposite end of the block. Something very fishy is going on here. I run through my mental list of suspicious characters I'd find in comics. This man is ragged and messy, like a scientist who lost his job and went rogue. Performing his own experiments on the streets. Biding his time until he can unleash his revenge on the city.

Mom comes back into the waiting room, wearing casual business-y clothes. She's put her hair up in a bun, so it looks more like it's slightly wet instead of sweaty. A middle-aged guy—Chris?—comes from the back and starts to chat with her. I glance outside.

"Nadia, you want to come with?" Mom asks. "Or stay out here?"

The raggedy man is ambling in this direction again, and now he has a small squirming animal under one arm. Without looking away, I tell Mom, "I'll stay here."

Footsteps leave the room. The receptionist answers a phone call. The man comes closer, talking to the small furry animal.

A dog. It's a small, scruffy dog. It yips and twists in his arms.

Where did that dog come from?

Is it his? Or did he just kidnap it?

Is he a mad scientist who does experiments on dogs?

He keeps muttering and stops a few doors down from this office. I put my head close to the glass for a better view. He's got the strange tool in his hand still, and while I watch he sits on the sidewalk, readjusts the dog, and then puts the tool against the dog's paw.

The dog starts yowling. Like, end-of-the-world, torturous-pain yowling.

I jump off the chair. The receptionist is still on her phone call and doesn't seem to notice anything. It doesn't matter if the dog is his or not—someone's got to save it!

I dash outside with no plan, no backup. I'm out of Eli's range. If this goes south—

The dog bites the man's hand and springs free. I dive forward and wrap my arms around it before it can run into the busy street. The dog yips and gives me a curious sniff.

The man, about six feet from me now, sighs. "Girl, if there was a medal for drama, you'd be the winner."

Cautiously, I sit up, still keeping ahold of the dog. She looks fine. Sort of dirty and scraggly but not hurt.

"Thanks for catching her, miss," the man says, pushing himself to his feet with a grunt. "She's a runner, that's for sure."

The dog wiggles too much for me to stand—I'm afraid she'll squirm right out of my arms. I check the distance to Synergy's door. Too far to leap inside without getting up first.

"What were you doing to her?" I ask instead, lifting my chin and staring at the man.

He blinks, then smiles. Some teeth are missing. Slowly, he squats down, still a bit away from me, and holds up the tool in his hand.

Dog nail clippers.

"This old lady"—he nods to the dog—"got some hip problems. Her nails get long and she gets achy. So I've got to trim 'em, which offends her quite a bit."

The dog has her eyes on the tool like it's the devil itself. I take her back right paw and manage to hold on long enough to see that about half the nails are clipped down while the other ones are overgrown. She yanks the paw away again with a dramatic whimper, even though I've done nothing but touch it.

A blush heats my cheeks.

For the first time, I look the man right in the face. His skin is wrinkly and tanned like leather. His amber eyes shine when he looks at the dog.

"I—I can help," I offer. "I've got a dog. I hold her when Dad cuts her nails, so—yeah."

He lowers his gaze again. "I'd appreciate that."

We shift out of the middle of the sidewalk, and I get his dog lying down. She gives big loud whimpers that could break a heart, and when the man touches the clippers to a nail, she wails with all the passion of an opera singer. I tighten my mouth to keep a smile down. It's both pitiful and . . . sort of funny.

"Try talking to her," the man tells me, speaking softly even though there's a whole concert of dog mourning between us. "Girl likes people talking."

I give it a go, but she doesn't pay me any attention. I try

making clicking noises, squeaky noises, any sort of weird sound that would have Wonder Dog curious. This dog just ignores me.

Finally, desperate, I give Eli's dove call a go. "Woo WOO ooo ooo ooo."

Her ears perk up. She stares at me, momentarily distracted. The man clips one nail.

"Woo WOO ooo ooo ooo," I try again. She whimpers, but sort of absentmindedly.

Between my dove calls and the man's quick work now that he's not wrestling a tornado of anxiety, it only takes a couple of minutes before he leans back with a triumphant, "There. Done."

I let the dog go and she springs up, wagging her tail so much her bottom jiggles. She greets both of us with kisses, like she's just been rescued from a desert island. I can't help giggling.

The man pulls a frayed leash out of his shopping cart and hooks it on the dog's collar. "Thank you, miss."

I give him a quick nod, but my face heats again. I feel like a total idiot for suspecting him of hurting his dog.

"I've gotta—go back to my mom," I say, scrambling up. "Um—have a nice day!"

I duck inside before he can respond and head straight to the bathroom. My skin burns. If that man had telepathy—if he could have read my thoughts when I first saw him—he'd know I didn't deserve any thanks. And I feel so embarrassed, I might as well have posted my evil-scientist theory on the wall.

After I splash cold water on my face, I slink back out. Mom's in the waiting room now, holding her bag with her bike clothes.

"Hey there," she says with a smile. "I've finished up. You ready for some Nicecream?"

"Sure." I move out of the way so she can go change. Through the window, I don't see the man anymore. Would Eli have thought those terrible things? Probably not. Heroes don't just assume stuff like that about people.

Mom changes into her biking clothes and we head out to the heat. I spot the man down by the end of the block—he's parked his grocery cart, with the dog tied to it, and is holding a cardboard sign.

"I think we deserve the biggest ice creams they'll give us," Mom says, beginning to pedal.

"Mm-hmm," I agree.

We ride in his direction. He gives me a nod. Mom doesn't

seem to notice—she checks the light and glides across the street without stopping.

I see his sign clearly for the first time. Big handwriting says: *Vet Needs Help*.

And the hand he holds it with has a small dog bite.

I slow down. My foot touches the pavement, almost all on its own, and I stop in front of him. A superhero would probably swoop in and carry him to a hospital. Maybe give him a home in their mansion. I can't do that—but I have to do something more than just hold his dog.

Bracing my legs so my bike won't fall over, I swing my backpack around and pull out the first aid kit. My hand brushes one of the fresh water bottles, and I grab it as well. I hold them both to him.

"Oh." He blinks at my hands. His fingers shaking, he takes the gifts. He smells like metro-station sweat, but when his gaze darts up at me, his amber eyes brighten.

I smile and he smiles back.

"Catch the light," he says, so soft I barely understand. He nods toward the street.

I turn around and see that the crosswalk is counting down. *Six, five* . . . I push off, give him a wave, and flick across to where my mom is waiting. She watches me with an odd look. When I catch up, she reaches over to brush back one of my braids.

"Nadia Quick," she says, "you might just be the coolest kid I know."

I shake my head. That's only because she hasn't met Eli.

Chapter 10

QUESTIONS UNANSWERED

We bike home, then I shower, change, and eat. Even after all that, it's still a few minutes before one thirty. I make my way to Eli's at a leisurely pace, doing my best to not be *too* ahead of time.

Mrs. B is walking toward her birdhouse, a bag of birdseed in her hand. I definitely can't go to Eli's yard while there are potential witnesses around. But before I can change course, she sees me.

She lifts her hand in a wave. "Good afternoon, Nadia. How are you doing?"

"Doing good." I come closer, watching the way she carefully lays out a trail of birdseed on the little wraparound porch. "I like your birdhouse."

"Thank you, dear. My husband made it for me." She smiles, a bit sadly. "Did you notice it's a replica of Mount Vernon—George Washington's house?"

I tilt my head and take another look. The birdhouse is long and white, with little windows and doors painted on. It has a red roof and a teeny tiny cupola—that's what they call the little tower that sticks out of the roof of an old building.

"That's really cool!" I say, peering into the bird-sized hole. "Is anything nesting in it?"

"No." She sighs. "Not a lot of birds have come by. Maybe I'll have more luck at my new place." She gives me a slight shrug. "James is helping me find something with a garden, or a balcony—so I can keep this and some of my flowers."

"Neat," I say, but I can't keep my eyes from sliding toward Eli's gate. It must be one thirty by now.

Mrs. B finishes putting out her birdseed. "Well, my dear, I think I'd better get back to packing. Don't stay out too long—this heat is something else!"

"Okay." I give her a thumbs-up. "Have a good day, Mrs. B."

"You too," she says, going back inside.

Perfect.

I rush over to the gate, giving our agreed-on call as I go. "Woo WOO ooo ooo ooo."

The gate opens, and Wonder Dog trots in ahead of me. Eli swings it shut quietly behind us, then squats to give Wonder's ears a scratch. Without looking up at me, he says, "Hello, Nadia."

"Hello, Eli, also known as Invisible Boy. What are you doing today?"

"Installing these." Eli holds up a small light, the sort people have next to driveways sometimes. He stands again, pushing his hoodie sleeves up over his elbows. Why someone would wear a hoodie during July is beyond me. That thick fabric must be twice as hot as my leggings. "Want to help?"

"Sure." I let Wonder off her leash and grab a handful of digging tools and spare lamps, following Eli down the path. I'm still not totally sure why a superhero spends all his time gardening. "Hey—how long have you lived here?"

"Two years," he answers. He already installed about half the lights before I arrived, so he kneels once we're well down the path. He takes a measuring tape from his pocket and starts checking the distance between the last light and where he'll put the next one.

"I never saw you before you saved Wonder." I sit across from him and pause. Trying to bend so he'll look me in the face, I add, "Thank you for that, by the way. Seriously."

His gaze starts coming up toward my face, then darts away. Avoiding eye contact. "I stay inside a lot. Or I'm back here."

"Oh." I pass him a hand shovel. I'm not buying that for a moment—as a superhero, he would obviously be on secret missions most of the time. But I'll play along. "Why?"

He shrugs.

"Is it because of Paddle Boy? 'Cause I'd totally understand if he's the reason." I wrinkle my nose. "*I'd* stay inside to avoid him."

Eli gives me a strange look. "Do you mean that boy who lives across the street?"

"Yeah. Kalvin or whatever."

"Why would you avoid him?"

"Because he's the worst."

Eli doesn't reply. A plane hums overhead, on its way to Ronald Reagan International Airport, and Eli and I both squint up to watch. I wonder where the people inside are going, and what they hope to find, and how they feel about it. I bet there are a ton of stories on every single flight.

A question pops into my head. "What do you want to be when you grow up?"

"When I grow up?" he repeats, like it's a weird idea.

"Right." I give him a look. "Don't you think about that?"

He doesn't answer right away. Then, suddenly, he says, "Teacher."

Not what I was expecting. "What would you teach?"

With a shrug, he pats the earth around one of the lights. "I don't know. Maybe math. I liked math."

"Eh, math's okay." I take the tape measure and count out one foot from the light, then stick a piece of mulch in the ground to mark the spot. "Where do you go to school?"

He scoots down to the new mark, adjusts the spot so it's a little farther from the stones, then starts digging. "I'm—I do school at home."

"But—who teaches you? I thought Candace has a job or something." At least, she never seems to be home when I'm over during the day. And I don't remember seeing her car in the driveway very often since I moved to this street. I guess she could teach him at night, but that's when she has her house parties.

"A . . . tutor." He shakes his shaggy hair out of his eyes. "What about you? What do you want to be?"

"An investigative journalist," I say without hesitation.

A grin flashes across his face. "You'd be good at that."

I busy myself marking the next place, hoping he can't see my grin. To the ground, I add, "I used to think about being a long-distance biker—like, the bicycle type, not the motorcycle one. My parents and I bike the Mount Vernon Trail every couple weeks. Sometimes even from here to Arlington Memorial Bridge and then all the way to DC."

"I used to have a bike," Eli says. He stands and wipes his dirty hands on his pants. The hole over his knee tightens on his skin for a moment, revealing crisscrossed white scars.

"Is that how you got those?" I ask, pointing.

He glances down and tugs the frayed fabric to cover the opening. "Um. Yeah."

"Hmm." I go back to measuring while he returns to the patio for more supplies. Wonder Dog trots after him, wagging her tail. I push some soggy leaves out of my way. Then, genius strikes. I grab a handful and duck behind a tree off the path.

When Eli returns, he stops and looks around for me. "Nadia?"

I jump out and lob the leaves at his face. The pile hits his arm (my aim is bad) and he blinks, surprised.

A laugh bursts out of me. "Got you!"

He stares for a moment, and just when I start to worry that he's upset, he sets down his supplies and snatches his own pile. I squeal, ducking my head behind my arms, and a handful of wet leaves splats onto my hair. There's a stick near my foot, and I take it, spinning on my heel and brandishing it like a sword.

"Ha!" I shout. The rotted wood sags in the middle and breaks without Eli even having to touch it.

He lifts his eyebrows.

"Hold on!" I search the ground for a worthy replacement. "I need a better sword!"

"Too bad I know where they are." Eli takes off, Wonder running after him.

I give chase. "Not fair!"

The path twists and turns, making the yard seem enormous. It feels like another world—one far away from the ordinary neighborhood. One where superheroes play and summer reigns and no evil dares enter.

Rounding a curve, I skid to a stop. In front of me, the shed stands in its quiet spot. Eli has vanished. Again.

Wonder Dog sniffs around, like she's lost him, too.

When I put my fingers to the shed door, it creaks open. Inside, everything is orderly, just like it was the night of the party. Not a single cobweb, not even any dust. But just like that night, there's no boy here.

"Surrender now, or face your doom."

I whip around. Eli's holding a long stick right in my face, eyes shining with excitement. It's like he's changed—no longer the kid whose gaze skirts away from mine, the one who hesitates before every decision. This is the boy who dove into the water after Wonder.

"You'll never take me alive!" I snatch a rake from the shed and knock his stick away. With a shout of challenge, I vault out the doorway at him. He dodges faster than I anticipated, and my foot catches on the stones at the edge of the path. I shoot headfirst into a bush.

"Nadia?" Eli asks. I hear him take a step closer. "Are you okay?"

I spit leaves out of my mouth and roll over, lifting my rake at the same time. I push the handle firmly against his chest. "Got you!"

One side of his mouth tilts up. "You did that on purpose?"

"Definitely," I lie, grinning.

He nudges the handle aside and moves back for distance. He twirls his stick sword in his hand—almost drops it— corrects his hold and extends it toward me. "Round two!"

But before we can begin, a timer somewhere in the house goes off. Wonder Dog gives a startled bark. Eli sags and lowers the stick.

"What's that?" I ask, not letting down my guard in case it's a trick.

"Nothing. But—I have to get back inside." He leans his stick against the shed wall. "I have to do some chores in there."

"Oh, well, I could help," I offer. Chores are not my first choice of activity, but if it means I get to learn more about Eli, then it would be worth it.

He shakes his head and takes my rake, setting it back in its place in the shed. "No, that's okay. Thanks, though."

I follow as he starts walking back to the gate. This visit has been way too short for any real progress. I kind of wonder if he planned that timer as an excuse to put off my investigation. "I can come back tomorrow, though, right?"

Eli hesitates. "I . . . guess."

I hook on Wonder Dog's leash, relieved. "Great. Okay. I'll see you then."

Eli shrugs and opens the gate for me. "Yeah, I—"

There's someone standing outside the gate.

We both freeze.

"I thought I heard noise back here." Paddle Boy, arms crossed, lifts one eyebrow. He looks from me to Eli. "Who are you?"

"Nothing! No one!" I say, way too loud. I shove Paddle Boy back and pull the gate—

Paddle Boy sticks his foot in my way and forces it open. He blinks. "Hold on. Where'd that boy go?"

I look, too. Eli has disappeared.

Exhaling in relief, I ask innocently, "What boy?"

"Ha-ha. Very funny." Paddle Boy glares at me but shuts the gate hard enough that the latch clangs. "Who was that kid? What's going on?"

"I don't see how that's any of your business." I lift my chin and march past him to the street. But of course, Paddle Boy follows.

"That's the boy I saw late at night," he says, maybe to me or maybe to himself. "How long has he been there? Did you ask him why he's outside super late?"

"Why were *you* out super late?" I shoot back.

Paddle Boy sniffs. "I wasn't *out*. I was playing Minecraft, and it was the weekend, so I'm *allowed* to be up late."

Of course it has something to do with video games. I decide to ignore him.

"Oh, jeez, the silent treatment?" He picks up his pace so he's glowering beside me. "So mature."

Still looking straight ahead, I say, "This is top secret and you don't get to know."

"Top—?" Paddle Boy groans in frustration. "*I'm* the one who gave you information about him at the park." I don't answer, and after a few minutes he mutters, "I thought maybe you'd changed."

My face heats, though I'm not sure why. I want him to stop asking questions. I want him to forget he ever saw Eli. I spin on my heel and point in his face. "Just because I saved your life doesn't mean I *like* you."

"Wow. Okay." He lifts his hands in surrender and turns the other way. "Whatever, Nadia."

I watch him leave.

Somehow, I feel worse than I have all day.

Chapter 11

UNINVITED GUEST CRASHES PARTY

rush to Eli's on Wednesday afternoon, desperate to explain. I can only hope he doesn't think that I actually *wanted* Paddle Boy to come—that I broke my promise and gave away the secret. Wonder Dog sniffs at a huge branch that's down in Mrs. B's front yard, but I pull her past without giving it more than a glance. If Eli thinks I'm a traitor, he might not even let me see him.

"Woo WOO ooo ooo ooo," I call as I come to a stop. The wooden fence stands massive, cutting me off from the world of superheroes and friendship and adventure. I barely breathe, waiting.

After an agonizing two minutes, a latch clicks and the gate swings ajar.

I push into the backyard and start my speech. "I am *so* sorry, but I told you he's the worst and—"

Eli's gaze flicks to me, and then something past my shoulder. He points.

I spin around.

Paddle Boy is standing behind me, in the gate's opening.

"The worst?" he repeats, one infuriating eyebrow raised. Then he shifts his attention to Eli. "Okay. Who are you?"

Eli's hands shake. He glances toward me—not my face— and his mouth parts, though no sound comes out.

I jump between the two of them, shielding Eli from Paddle Boy's view. I'll buy time, and Eli can escape. "You *followed* me?"

"Well, it was clear I wasn't getting information any other way." Paddle Boy leans back and folds his arms.

"You aren't allowed to be here," I snap, putting my fists on my hips. Wonder Dog ruins the effect by wagging her tail and giving Paddle Boy's shorts a friendly sniff. I tug the leash, but she ignores me. Trying to maintain my tone of command, I add, "You—you should leave."

"Is this a secret club or something?" Paddle Boy's eyes light up with interest.

"Ugh." I barely keep in a groan. "I guess. Sure. But you aren't invited."

"Last I checked, this isn't your house." Paddle Boy moves to go around me, but I shift into his way again. He rolls his eyes. "Well, what do I need to do to *get* invited?"

"You have to promise to tell no one," Eli says behind me.

I whirl in surprise. Eli is still totally visible, his skin pale and his eyes dark and his hands in his hoodie pockets.

He should get out of here. He should disappear.

"Okay," Paddle Boy agrees.

"What?" I demand to Eli. I wave my hand in Paddle Boy's direction. "We can't just let *him* in here!"

"He already *is* here," Eli points out with a sharp glance at me.

"I promise I won't tell a soul." Paddle Boy crosses his heart. "And I'll be way better than Nadia at sneaking around."

I gape. *The nerve!*

Paddle Boy steps past me to get a look at the yard. "So what's the deal here? You live with Candace?"

Eli nods silently.

"What's your name?" Paddle Boy asks.

I jump in before Eli can answer. "The Invisible Boy!"

They both look at me, confused.

"I'm Lightning Lane," I add, lowering my voice. "Wonder Dog is Wonder Dog. I have the power of stopping time, and Eli is invisible and also can fly. Wonder Dog has hyper speed."

"Okay . . ." Paddle Boy frowns. "So it's a secret superhero club? What should my superpower be?"

Smashing paddles, I think.

But I keep quiet. We are in the Red Zone here, full-on Emergency Level 1. A supervillain has infiltrated Eli's hideout. It's time to play nice—until I can get rid of Paddle Boy without any property damage.

Think. I don't really *know* that much about Paddle Boy, other than the paddle incident. We go to the same middle school, we're even in the same grade, but we never hang out. He might have information about me from spying on my mom's blog, but I'm not even sure I could name his favorite color.

"Well—coming up with a superpower is easy for *most* people," I explain to him, biting back my annoyance. "You pick a hobby or a favorite thing you already have—like, how I'm basically a reporter—and then you add a superpower that would make it easier. I can stop time so I can take notes."

Paddle Boy frowns. Impatient, I motion for him to have a go.

"Um . . ." He rubs his head. "I like . . . Minecraft."

I try not to roll my eyes.

"I like making cities on it. I've made a replica of DC—for a school project, but it was pretty fun."

"That does sound kind of okay," I admit reluctantly. "So—what would make you better at doing that?"

"High-speed Wi-Fi." His eyes widen with delight. "I could be Wi-Fi Man. I make my own Wi-Fi wherever I go, connecting gamers everywhere. And," he adds, looking sheepish, "y'know, saving innocent people and stuff."

Man might be a big huge stretch. But if it keeps him happy, so be it. "Fine. You are now Wi-Fi Man."

"Sweet." He smiles, a little tentatively.

No one says anything. Eli is still standing basically frozen, stiff and wary. I want to get him away from Paddle Boy and explain that I'm coming up with a plan to make this right. But Paddle Boy acts totally comfortable, examining the patio like he was invited over.

Somewhere nearby, a door closes. Eli hears it, too, and stands up straighter.

Paddle Boy turns back to us. "So what do you guys—?"

"Shh." Eli motions him to be quiet.

We listen.

There's a soft little crying sound. "Ohhhh!"

It's coming from Mrs. B's property.

I tiptoe to the fence and find a crack between the boards. Through it, I can see part of Mrs. B's house and front yard. She goes to a fallen tree branch—which is nearly as big as she is tall—and kneels. Another little sound comes from her— almost like a whimper.

Paddle Boy nudges me over so he can see, too. I elbow him in the ribs. Eli takes a place by the gate hinges, where there's another gap.

"Grandma?" James's voice, coming from the direction of the front door. He breathes in sharply enough that I can hear it, and a second later he jogs into my view of the branch. "Is it—?"

Mrs. B lifts something out of the tangle of leaves. Scraps of white and red wood.

The birdhouse her husband made her.

"We can fix it," James says, squatting and taking one of the pieces. "I'm sure it could be repaired if we . . ."

Mrs. B shakes her head. I can't see her face from here, but her voice sounds wispy. "It's all right, hon." He opens his mouth to argue, but she puts a hand on his arm. "I don't . . . I don't want to fuss about it. I'll be fine. Just give me a moment."

James hesitates. "Well—here, I'll move the branch over to

the side of the road. We'd better call someone to come take it away."

While he shifts and grunts and drags the branch, Mrs. B collects the fragments of broken birdhouse. Even the wooden pole it stood on is crushed. When she has her arms full of everything, she walks toward Eli's yard. He steps away from the gate, so softly he doesn't make a sound. I hold my breath but keep watching.

Quietly, she places the wood in the recycling bin on this side of her house. She pauses for a moment, looking down at it, and then lowers the lid. She stands there, her hand trembling as she rests it on the top. Two big tears slide down her cheeks.

James walks over from the yard, brushing his palms on his pant legs. "Are you sure you don't want me to—?"

Mrs. B makes a swipe at her cheeks and swivels with a quick smile. "I'm sure. You're doing so much already." She takes his arm and walks toward the front door. "I think we should have some lemonade and get back to work on the closets . . ."

A moment later, I hear the front door close. I move back and bump into Paddle Boy.

"Sorry," he mutters, getting out of the way.

Both of us are solemn, but when Eli faces me, his expression is eager. "Can you get those pieces, Nadia?"

"Um, sure." I pass Wonder Dog's leash to him and slip

through the gate. The recycling is in a smallish rolling trash can, and when I open it, the pieces are splayed out over some old cardboard. I grab whatever I can carry—which isn't quite all of it—but before I turn away, shoes shuffle beside me. I glance over my shoulder.

Paddle Boy has followed me—again.

Mutely, I pass him my handful of scraps, then lean back over to get the last of them. At least I'll only have to make one trip. Inside the garden, we put all the pieces down on the patio, and Eli starts to sort through them. The crumbled remains of the birdhouse look pitiful. I glance at Paddle Boy and narrow my eyes. This wouldn't be the first time something in the neighborhood got smashed.

But before I can put together a solid theory for how he might have destroyed another precious neighborhood item, Paddle Boy asks, "Can we fix it?"

"What?" I blurt.

"Mr. B made that for her." He crouches down across from Eli. "She told me at the house party. It's really important."

"I know that," I reply, crossing my arms.

Softly, Eli adds, "He gave it to her right before he got sick. As an anniversary surprise."

Well, I didn't know that. But Eli's been around longer than both Paddle Boy and me.

Paddle Boy picks up the tiny cupola. Somehow, it's still in one piece. "So—do you think we can fix it?"

"The ends are mostly intact," Eli says, almost to himself. "That—and the little piece you're holding—would be the hardest part, so—maybe. I have the tools. If I had the right supplies, I think I could put this back together."

"I have some scrap wood," Paddle Boy says. "We could use that for the pieces we need to replace."

"I can get paint," I offer. "I have a ton left over from an art project."

Eli nods slowly. "Okay. Let's try."

I look from him to Paddle Boy. I've never worked alongside a supervillain.

This will be interesting.

Chapter 12

STORMS IN THE FORECAST

We all agreed that we shouldn't meet on the Fourth of July. Eli said Candace is having a big party, and Paddle Boy is supposed to hang out with his mom, and I know Mom, Dad, and Aunt Lexie will be expecting card games and grilling. So—after a typical day of family activities, capped by fireworks—it's Friday before I can head over to Eli's again. I fill my backpack with old paints and brushes. Music blasts down the hall, coming from the ex–guest room/new studio. Mom and Dad have been working in there most of the morning to the tune of extremely loud seventies and eighties songs. Not my favorite, to be honest. It's about one o'clock now, so too early for visiting Eli, but I don't think I can take much more of this. I grab Wonder Dog's leash and go downstairs.

She's flopped over on the hardwood floor, looking about as sick of this music as I feel.

I hold up the leash. "Want to go on a walk?"

Wonder Dog scrambles up in a burst of fur, mouth wide in a doggy smile. I snap the leash on her harness and slip outside. The air is thick with a humid, leafy smell that means a storm is coming. We wander around the yard, and Wonder pees in the normal places. Though I try to move slowly and take plenty of time, we wind up by the big old pine tree on the far side within five minutes.

Our canoe rests on the lowest branches, upside down so it won't gather rainwater. I grab a stick and clear out some spiderwebs by the seats. Dad and I haven't gone out on Little Hunting Creek or the Potomac River since the Paddle Boy incident. My parents have promised to replace the paddle, but neither of them has remembered long enough to go online and actually buy a new one. Between Dad's Pentagon job and my end-of-the-school-year workload, I'm not sure that we really would have been canoeing much anyway. Now that it's summer, we could probably go on weekends—if we had two paddles. It's clumsy and hard to navigate with only one.

Looking at the canoe's faded pale green paint makes me long to pull it down, flip it over, and take it to the water.

Instead, I wrap my arms around a low branch and walk my feet up the trunk. Wonder Dog waits down below. Once I'm up in the thick of the branches, I throw her leash over another branch and hoist her up beside me. Wonder Dog swings contentedly in her soft harness until I pull her onto the branch. She wags her tail and licks my cheek.

While Wonder tests the branches around her to see if she'd like to climb a bit, I look out at Little Hunting Creek. The ospreys are napping in their nest. Between Little Hunting Jr.—where James fell in—and the nesting pole is our small peninsula.

Something has washed up on the far side of the peninsula. I sit up straighter and push one of the branches out of my way. My heart gives a leap.

It's a long wooden pole.

The perfect size for a birdhouse stand.

I check my phone—1:25. In the winter, I can cross the frozen water to the peninsula, but right now the connecting part is five inches deep in mud, bramble, and thorns. No time for that now. I slide off the branch and lower Wonder Dog down. Within five minutes we're outside Eli's gate. Paddle Boy walks up, too. I give him a civil nod, then cup my hands to my mouth. "Woo WOO ooo ooo ooo."

After a few seconds, the gate swings open. "Hello."

"Hi!" I hurry inside and bend to unclip Wonder Dog's leash. "Guess what I just found. On the peninsula behind my house—"

I stand up and look at Eli. He's always sort of shaggy and wild, but today he looks flat-out exhausted. The skin around his eyes is so dark, it's almost like he was in an Old West saloon fight. I blink in surprise. "Are you . . . okay?"

"Yes." He closes the gate quietly, then bends down to pet Wonder Dog. She sniffs his jeans and gives his ankle a little bop. He must have been out patrolling, fighting crime, saving cats from trees; he could clearly use a rest.

"I brought some wood scraps and glue and stuff," Paddle Boy says, holding up a plastic bag. "Have you ever built a birdhouse before, Invisible Boy?"

"Only invisible ones." Eli's mouth quirks on one side, but stops short of a smile. He leads us over to the patio, where he's set out the salvageable pieces of the old birdhouse, along with nails, a hammer, and a handsaw. "I have a pretty good idea how to do it, though."

"Well, Wi-Fi Man to the rescue, then—because I have tutorials." Paddle Boy sits beside the pile and pulls up some videos on his phone screen.

Eli and I move to watch, while Wonder Dog sniffs around the bushes. Someone's stomach rumbles loudly—it isn't mine, and Paddle Boy glances up like he's surprised, so I'm guessing it is Eli. Again. It's odd that he doesn't eat lunch earlier, instead of waiting until after he gardens.

The video ends. Paddle Boy dumps his bag of stuff out on the patio. "So I think these can work for the walls." He selects two longer pieces. A bottle labeled *Wood Glue* and another hammer fall out, too. "If we do it like the tutorial, we should glue the pieces to the base, let it dry, and then use nails for extra support."

Eli nods and rummages through the other scraps. "I'll need to trim those pieces and the roof before we start building."

I take out my paints and brushes. "Once they're sized right, I can get painting."

We split off into teams. Eli and Paddle Boy work on sawing the wood—which means Eli saws and Paddle Boy watches in case he hurts himself. I pull out a paper plate and start mixing paints, trying to find the perfect bright red that will match the original color. Once the pieces are all laid out and ready, the boys begin assembling and I start on the roof.

Now that no one is working with a sharp blade, I tell them about seeing the pole and my plan to get it tomorrow or Sunday and bring it on Monday. "It would be a lot easier with a canoe," I mention, with a look at Paddle Boy, "but I think I can manage."

Paddle Boy's ears turn red. "Well—Invisible Boy could just fly over and get it, right? That'd be the easiest option."

"Sorry, I take weekends off." Eli shrugs and grins suddenly, like it's a hilarious joke. To me, Eli adds, "Hold on—why do I have invisibility powers, again?"

Now it's my turn to blush. "If you're going to have flying powers in the Washington, DC, area, you'd need *some* kind of cover to avoid being shot down as an unidentified flying object."

"Does his invisibility also change body heat?" Paddle Boy asks. "'Cause otherwise he might still show up on radars and stuff."

"Maybe I could also be really fast?" Eli suggests. He presses one gluey edge to another.

"Or maybe you and Nadia could, like, team up." Paddle Boy holds the two sides together and Eli starts putting glue on another one. "If you can stop time, Nadia, can you extend the power to other people? Then you could jump on Eli's back, stop time, and he could fly you both into the city."

"That could work," I admit. Paddle Boy is better at this than I expected.

There's a pause while Eli puts together another side of the birdhouse. Paddle Boy shifts so he can give it support. He asks, "So, is Candace your mom?"

Quietly, Eli answers, "She's my aunt."

I feel a little thick for never actually asking that before. But it makes sense that with his standard-hero troubled parental past, he would be with an aunt. I need to figure out where his dad is, too—or what happened to him—but perhaps when Eli is more talkative.

"What school do you go to?" Paddle Boy asks, moving his foot over to support the third side of the birdhouse.

"He's homeschooled," I cut in. There's no reason for Paddle Boy to grill him. Not that I haven't grilled him, too. But it's annoying coming from Paddle Boy.

Paddle Boy glances from me to Eli. "Oh. Have you always been homeschooled?"

Eli hesitates. "No. I went to a public school until I was in seventh grade."

"What school?" he asks.

"It wasn't around here." Eli taps two of the edges to get them better aligned. "But I liked it. There was one teacher, Mr. Colvin, who was really nice. He had a hedgehog named Skywalker, and he would have us practice reading with it."

"I've never had a hedgehog," I say enviously. "Though my kindergarten class had a hamster."

"Mine just had hermit crabs." Paddle Boy shudders. "They

would crawl underground to molt and—well, once it started smelling, you knew they weren't coming out again."

I scrunch up my nose. "That's awful!"

Paddle Boy nods. "Yeah, basically."

"Okay, that should take a few minutes to dry," Eli interrupts. The fourth side of the birdhouse is now attached, with Paddle Boy holding them all together. Eli rocks back on his heels. "I need to get smaller nails from the shed. I'll be right back."

I jump to my feet, put my hand on his shoulder, and say, "Time freeze!"

Eli looks up at me, confused. Paddle Boy holds completely still. Not even breathing.

I try to hold in a giggle. "Come on, Invisible Boy! We'll get the nails and be back before he knows what happened!"

Smiling, Eli stands and runs toward the shed. I glance back at the patio while I follow. Paddle Boy is sitting motionless, and Wonder Dog wanders over to sniff his ear. Paddle Boy shakes with a silent laugh.

"Hey," I say to Eli in a low voice. "I am really, really sorry about P—about Wi-Fi Man finding you."

"It's . . . not actually that bad." Eli opens the shed door and goes inside. "I guess superheroes can always use more allies, yeah?"

I'm still not convinced that Paddle Boy is an ally. But he definitely doesn't seem as evil as I originally suspected. Eli takes a small box of nails and we return together. Wonder Dog is pawing at Paddle Boy's leg now, making worried woofs. He has his eyes closed tight and his mouth pinched together to keep from smiling.

"Unfreeze!" I say.

Paddle Boy exhales a whoosh of air and blinks at us. Eyes widening in surprise, he says, "Wow! You got those so fast!"

Eli bursts into laughter.

I plop down in my spot and start applying a second layer of paint to the roof. "Just the way I work."

Overhead, the clouds darken and a breeze rustles the treetops. I finish the roof and move on to the walls, once Eli has hammered everything together. Paddle Boy pulls up a photo of Mount Vernon on his phone, and I do my best to replicate the windows and doors. Birds start swooping from branch to branch, and Wonder Dog presses her side against me. I keep working, kind of hoping that if I ignore the signs, the storm will just skip over us. Thunder rumbles in the distance.

A big drop of rain lands on Paddle Boy's hand. He tilts his head back and checks the sky. "I think I'd better be getting home."

Eli nods. "We've done all we can today, without a pole to

stand it on. And I need to—do some other chores." He stands, pulling his hoodie's hood up over his hair. Rain peppers down on us, throwing little flecks of wet across our clothes.

"So, are we meeting up again tomorrow?" Paddle Boy asks.

"No, tomorrow is Saturday. You can't come on weekends." Eli smiles. "Remember? I take weekends off."

I open my mouth to ask more questions, but Eli is firm.

"If you want to come over, you can only come during the week, at one thirty, and you can't tell anyone about me. Those are the rules."

Paddle Boy shrugs. I nod reluctantly. I already agreed to these terms, but I wish Eli would explain them.

I help Eli gather up the remaining scraps of the old birdhouse and stick my paints in my backpack. Paddle Boy makes quick work of scooping his things into the plastic bag. The air flashes with distant lightning, like someone taking a picture, though I don't hear any thunder this time. Wonder Dog pins back her ears and leans her shoulder against my knee.

"It's okay," I say, snapping on her leash. I take one final look around—everything is cleaned up and put away. Eli's stored the work-in-progress birdhouse in his shed. No one would be able to tell that we were even here.

Eli goes to the gate and opens it for Paddle Boy. The rain starts coming down more steadily.

Paddle Boy glances at Eli. "Think your invisibility can get me out of the secret lair without being spotted?"

"Can do." Eli gives him a thumbs-up. "But you'd better hurry."

Paddle Boy salutes with two fingers, then dashes out to the street. I watch, half expecting him to disappear into the rain. But no, I can see him jumping over puddles, trying to beat the storm. Just like I can see Eli standing next to me in his red hoodie.

I've been working on the scoop of a lifetime: a superhero living in suburban Virginia. But all signs indicate that I have not uncovered a superhero *or* a supervillain. Just two boys who I prodded into playing.

Paddle Boy goes through his front door. The raindrops are bigger and thicker now, a curtain between me and the rest of the street. I shiver in my soaked shirt, even though it isn't very cold. I think I should feel disappointed. But I don't feel sad at all. I turn to Eli—he's looking past me, one hand on the gate.

He opens and closes his mouth, but doesn't say anything.

I knock his shoulder with mine. "Hey," I say, but he doesn't look at me. "Stay dry!"

His hood is drenched and his hair sticks to his forehead in raggedy clumps. He doesn't smile. So quiet I almost can't hear over the rain, he asks, "You'll come back?"

"Yeah." I nod, keeping my voice light. "On Monday. I promise."

For a second, he glances up—almost at my face, but not quite. His eyes glimmer with a faint sheen, like the flash of leaves when they turn over before a storm. He gives me a single nod. Then he moves to close the gate.

As I leave, that look plays through my head over and over.

Chapter 13

HOW (NOT) TO GO VIRAL

By Sunday, I'm still thinking about that look. About the way Eli never leaves his yard, unless it's to rescue Wonder Dog or me. About how he *is* weirdly invisible, for someone who doesn't have superpowers.

If he isn't an actual superhero, all the strange things about him get even stranger.

I flip through some of my favorite Superman comics, reading everything I can about Clark Kent. Was he ever scared? So far, I mostly notice him being worried for other people (especially Lois Lane). Sometimes he seems overwhelmed or uncertain. But never outright afraid.

Was Eli afraid when I left him at the gate on Friday

afternoon? I don't know. I can't tell. But something has shifted in me. Something doesn't feel right.

There's a knock on my bedroom door, and Mom looks in. She is wearing makeup and has her hair fixed into its extra-curly style. "Hey, Dia, I'm about to do my big announcement. Do you want to be in the video?"

"Um . . ." Pretty much the last thing I want is to be a prop in Mom's live reveal of her new podcast studio. But Mom grins at me and fidgets with her phone and almost bounces. She's so excited that I shrug and get to my feet. "Okay, I guess."

"Perfect!" Mom jumps over to my dresser and pulls out a long purple tunic-y shirt and leggings covered in yellow flowers. "Want to change into this? And maybe we could run a brush through your hair?"

I sigh but go through the motions of getting ready. It's almost five, so I think Mom's planning a pre-dinner live-stream. She flits around adjusting things—making sure my hair isn't tucked behind my ears, picking up one of Wonder's dog toys from the hallway, checking the lighting on her phone over and over. I'm not sure I've ever seen Mom this nervous about a livestream.

Dad comes out of their bedroom, dressed in a polo shirt and his camera-ready dark wash jeans instead of the washed-out, oil-splattered frayed shorts he usually wears on his days off.

I smile. "You got recruited, too?"

He laughs, a little loudly. Almost like *he's* nervous, too. "Well, technically I had a part in the surprise."

"Okay, everyone get set. Go stand by the door." Mom points us toward the ex–guest room and herds Wonder Dog downstairs.

Dad and I exchange a shrug and move to that end of the hallway. He has his right hand closed and his thumb taps against his finger.

Mom comes back. "You both ready?"

I tug on my hair. It feels weird without the normal two braids. "Sure."

"Yep," Dad replies, shifting his weight.

"Remember to face the camera," she says. "Nadia, I'll lead you in, with me walking backward, yeah? I want your reaction to be the focus—the moment when you see it for the first time. Then I'll pan around and show everyone. And Richard, you follow and then stand to the side so I can get your reaction last."

A kid's reaction to a podcast studio seems a bit odd to me, but my mom's done weirder stuff. Maybe she's afraid this is going to be a boring reveal, and she thinks that if I'm in the shot, people will be more interested.

A horrible thought pops into my head. Paddle Boy's mom is probably watching this.

Which means Paddle Boy might be watching.

I want to groan and crawl back to my room.

But right then, Mom holds up her fingers to count down. "Okay, and we're live in three . . . two . . . one!"

She fixes a smile on her face and holds it while she clicks record. There is officially no escape.

"Hello, Quicklings!" Mom says in her slightly fake, on-camera voice. "I am *so* excited to share my big announcement with you in just a few minutes, but I want to give folks time to show up. Shout-out to Jessica in California—great to have you join us, Jessica!" This goes on for a bit—Mom saying hi to various people who are leaving comments, and counting off whenever we round up to a milestone in viewers. Fifty, two hundred, six hundred by the first five minutes.

The whole time, Dad keeps fidgeting with his fingers, so much that I think he might be sending me Morse code. But if he is, it translates to something like, "*Au5qizz4*."

"All right! Everyone else is just going to have to catch this on replay." Mom winks at her phone. "Today I'm joined by my wonderful daughter, Nadia. She doesn't know what lies beyond this door, either, so you'll get to see her reaction as it happens! Say hello, Nadia!" Mom swaps the camera view so it'll show me. I stand up straighter and try to smile. It's creepy that somewhere six hundred people are watching me—and mortifying that one of them might be Paddle Boy. "Richard is also here," Mom says, swinging the camera up to get a shot of Dad waving. "But he's been in on this the whole time, so he's a spoiler just waiting to happen."

Dad opens his mouth, like he's going to say something.

"No hints!" She grins and turns the camera on me while she walks backward toward the door, reaching down with a free hand to push it open. "Okay, everyone. Now's the moment you've all been waiting for!"

She backs into the room, and I follow, trying to look excited for my mom's new studio. But as soon as I step in, something becomes clear.

I've got this story wrong.

The room isn't a studio.

It's a nursery.

A crib sits against one wall, a bookshelf with slim spines and baskets of baby supplies is tucked against another. Peachy pink and soft yellow decorations cover everything. Twinkle lights are strung around the top of the ceiling. Folksy stuffed animals smile from cubbies, and a mobile of the solar system spins slowly in the air.

Mom's not getting a new office.

She's having a baby.

Mom's voice buzzes around the back of my head. Asking questions? Prompting me to say something? But I can't hear over the rush of blood in my ears. My thoughts spin. I'm getting a sibling! A girl, it looks like. How soon? Can I name it? (Lois. No, no—Lucy, like Lois Lane's sister.)

I turn toward Mom, opening my mouth to ask, and find myself staring right into her phone's camera lens.

The excitement drains into a deep, crazy disappointment.

"Well?" Mom asks, grinning behind her screen. "What do you think of my *studio*?"

I close my mouth. My face burns. My thoughts don't want to translate into words, and all of it is a tangled mess in my head. *Say something!* I yell at myself while I stare stupidly at the camera. *Say anything!*

"I'm telling you all, I've never seen my daughter this speechless." Mom laughs. Dad, behind her now, chuckles. "Come on, Dia. What's your first impression?"

My voice comes out soft, almost toneless. "You didn't tell me?"

"What's that, honey? Speak up so we can all hear."

This time, my voice is harder. Louder. "You didn't tell me."

"That's why we call it a surprise!" Mom straightens and switches the camera back onto herself. Dad leans into the frame, still smiling. "So, everyone, I'm sorry for keeping you all in the dark! Richard and I were just as shocked as Nadia here when we found out a few months ago. But you saw it here first—the Quicks are having a baby girl!"

I stare and stare and stare. The room is beautiful, perfect. My parents are so happy. And I feel like I'm sinking into the floor. Like someone's scooped out my insides and filled my body with heavy black sludge. A big, wild sadness has swallowed me so deep that I can't even tell why it's here, or where it came from, or why my eyes won't focus and it hurts to breathe.

Mom circles the room, narrating as she goes. Dad points out things and poses by them like a model in a TV game show. Why didn't they tell me? Shouldn't I have been the first one to know?

Then suddenly the camera is back in front of me, and Mom's saying, "Let's see if Nadia here has anything—" And she stops. "Oh, Dia! Why are you crying?"

And just like that, it's a thousand times worse.

My face isn't just hot. My eyes aren't just unfocused.

I'm crying.

In front of over five hundred strangers.

And I don't even know why!

Before my mom can get a second more of footage for her blog, I turn on my heel and run. I run so fast, my socks skid over the floor when I turn the corner to my room. I throw myself inside and slam the door behind me. Then I crawl into my closet and sit on my smelly shoes and pull the door closed.

That way, no one will hear if I cry. Not even on a live-stream.

Chapter 14

CITIZENS POWERLESS AGAINST MORTIFICATION

I stay in my room all afternoon and most of the evening. Mom and Dad try to talk to me through the door, but I won't answer. I don't want to talk about it. I don't even want to think about it. Instead, I sit on the floor against my bed and read *Showcase Presents: Superman Family*, the old—and very weird—comics from forever ago. Somehow reading about Lois Lane nearly getting tricked into marriage with a perfect guy who turns out to be a robot who turns out to be remote controlled by an alien makes me feel a tiny bit better.

Eventually, Mom and Dad say they're going to "give me space" and stop trying. I only crack my door open to accept dinner. But even then, I won't look at them or speak to them.

Monday comes. I spend all morning in my room, too, but after a while I'm hungry and tired of old-version Lois Lane falling out windows. I make myself wait until the clock on my dresser says twelve thirty, then I pull on fresh clothes and sneak downstairs. I promised I'd figure out a way to get that pole for the birdhouse. And, more important, I promised Eli I would come today.

I get all the way to the kitchen before Wonder Dog gives an excited bark and runs up to greet me.

"Traitor," I whisper.

Wonder Dog wags her tail and doggy-grins.

Mom follows right behind her. "Nadia! You're out!" She gives me an uncertain smile. "Are you okay? Do you want to talk about—"

"I just want to take Wonder on a walk," I say, not exactly looking at her.

Mom hesitates. "Dia, are you upset about the baby? Or—?"

I don't answer, stuffing an apple into my backpack.

Mom opens her mouth to say something else, but I zip my backpack, hook the leash to Wonder's harness, and rush outside. The humid air drapes over everything like a thick blanket. I let Wonder Dog pee in her usual spot, then head to the peninsula. Low tide exposes the part that connects with my yard, making it possible to slog through the thick mud. I tie Wonder to the pine tree and start to pull off my shoes. Barefoot, I might step on some thorns—but this mud will slurp a shoe right off, and sometimes it doesn't show up again.

A voice calls out behind me.

"Hey—Nadia!"

The voice of the *last* person I want to see.

I turn slowly. Paddle Boy is hurrying toward me from the street, carrying something long and narrow wrapped in packing paper. My face heats. I don't want to fight with him or be around him or watch his stupid expression change from relief to pity. I want to run as fast as I can in the other direction—let the mud swallow me whole. But my feet won't move.

"I—um—" Paddle Boy stops in front of me and moves the wrapped thing behind his back. "I'm sorry about . . ."

He watched the livestream! My skin goes from hot to surface-of-the-sun scorching. And for some dumb reason, my eyes start to sting, and my lungs tighten, and I'm spiraling impossibly into a situation somehow *more* humiliating. I clench my hands into fists around my shoe, pushing back against the wave of frustration that wants to explode out of me.

"My mom watched it," he adds quickly. "I didn't—I went into a different room. But Mom told me what happened. She said she was glad your mom deleted the video."

I stare at him. "What?"

"After it went live, your mom took it down." He shrugs. "I mean—it might exist somewhere, 'cause nothing is ever really *gone* off the internet. But it's not on your mom's pages anymore. Anyway—um . . . that seemed pretty uncool."

"Yeah," I agree, not sure what else to say. "It was."

He stands awkwardly for a moment, and then seems to remember the wrapped thing in his hand and holds it out to me. Wonder Dog backs away, unsure.

But I get a good look, and my heart does a flip.

The package is shaped like a paddle.

"This is for you," he says.

I drop my shoe and tear off the brown paper. Sure enough, I'm holding a canoe paddle. A *nice* canoe paddle—light and sturdy with a streak of shiny dark wood down the center.

"I hope it's okay." Paddle Boy shifts on his feet. He points to the blade—the wide part at the bottom. "I added that."

I turn it so I can see. Under the paddle logo, there's a sticker that looks like a street sign. It says *Lois LN*. A grin wants to break onto my face, but I will the corners of my mouth to stay down. The world's turned inside out and I don't know how to act.

"I actually got it after the—the incident," he says, sticking his hands in his pockets. "But you, ah . . . We didn't really . . . hang out or anything so I just . . . didn't exactly give it to you. I didn't realize how important—"

Somehow, words swim up to the top of my brain, and I blurt, "Why *did* you break my paddle?"

He turns red. "I didn't know it was yours—I thought someone just left it by the creek." He points up at the canoe in the branches. "I mean, this *could* be abandoned. So—I picked up the paddle, but—there was a bee. It came right at me and I tried to swat it with the paddle and . . . I missed. Hit the tree. And the paddle broke."

I blink. "Oh."

"Yeah." He ducks his head.

That wasn't the nefarious scheme I expected all this time. It actually sounds like something I might do.

It looks like I've gotten all my scoops wrong. My mom's surprise. Eli's powers. Even Paddle Boy's crime, which I saw with my own eyes. I'm not an ace reporter—I don't even deserve to enter the Junior Journalists Contest.

"So. Do you want to go get that pole?" Paddle Boy asks. He clears his throat. "I figured now we could use your canoe."

"I—um—" I clear my throat, then I bend to slip on my shoe again. "Have you ever canoed before?"

He shakes his head. "Can you teach me?"

I lean the new paddle against the tree and reach up into the branches. "It's not that hard. Give me a hand with this."

Together, we leverage the canoe down and carry it to Little Hunting Jr. I run to the garage and come back with two life jackets and our one old paddle. I'm too embarrassed to admit I'd hid it there for safety, so I pass it to Paddle Boy—Kenny—without saying anything.

I untie Wonder Dog's leash and let her climb in with me. I take the back seat, Wonder settles in the middle, and Kenny wobbles his way to the front. Once he sits down and the canoe stops rocking, I push us off with the new paddle. It slides through the water soft and quiet, and the handle fits perfectly in my palm.

Kenny catches on, eventually, and kind of helps out. When we circle the peninsula to the other side, he's the one who climbs into the mud and pulls the pole free. Between us, we lay it down in the hull of the canoe. Then we return to my yard—a fifteen-minute trip in all, when it would have taken me a lot longer and involved a lot more mess if I'd gone over land.

By one thirty, we're outside Eli's gate, the pole balanced between our shoulders. It's only about five feet long, I'd guess, but it is way easier to carry with someone's help than it would have been alone. I still don't know what I think about Kenny and me being on the same side. But I don't feel like I'm going to explode with frustration and my eyes aren't stinging for the first time today.

I give the signal, and a moment later Eli opens the gate for us.

"We bring a pole!" I announce, marching in victoriously. Wonder Dog darts ahead of me to give Eli's hands a lick.

"Perfect." A smile turns the corner of Eli's mouth, but it fades as quickly as it appeared. He swings the gate shut behind us. "The birdhouse is pretty much done. If we put this in the back, I can do the final steps tonight."

Kenny frowns. "Why do we need to wait?"

"I have to finish cleaning up after the Fourth of July parties." Eli rubs the side of his neck. "I didn't get it done earlier. And—if you let me assemble the birdhouse, I can do it without anyone seeing." He lifts his eyebrows. "Invisibility powers, you know."

"Okay . . ." Kenny sounds as uncertain as I feel.

"Well, where should we put this?" I ask.

Eli leads the way to the very, very, very back of the yard and nods toward the fence. Once we lay it down, he covers it in leaves.

"Invisibility activated," he murmurs.

I don't really get why Eli wants the pole to be invisible. But . . . maybe he's just being extra thorough about the surprise.

Either way, he's heading back to the patio before Kenny and I can do more than exchange a shrug. I unhook Wonder Dog's leash and follow. He's barefoot, and still wearing his hoodie, though it's hot and sticky even in the shade.

One end of the patio has smudges of black over the stone. I'm guessing this is where some of Candace's party guests set off fireworks. Eli points. "I need to scrub that off. I should have gotten it done yesterday, but . . ." He trails off and then shakes his head. "Anyway, it'd be a lot of help if . . ."

"Sure, we'll help." I plant my hands on my hips in a superhero stance. "No task is too small for Lightning Lane."

"Or Wi-Fi Man," Kenny adds. "But, ah, actually . . ."

I give him a look. Is he seriously going to bail because we're scrubbing floors? His face reddens.

"I can't actually stay today," he explains quickly. "I just wanted to help get the pole—but I've got to go back home. My dad's supposed to come pick me up during his lunch break. We're doing a late Fourth of July celebration 'cause he had duty over the holiday."

"Oh." I suppose that could be considered a legitimate, not-just-getting-out-of-chores excuse. "Okay. See you tomorrow?"

"More like Friday, probably." He waves, jogging toward the gate. "If you guys need any Wi-Fi Man magic, just fly by my dad's apartment!"

"The one by the Iwo Jima Memorial?" I remember from our conversation at the party.

"Right! It's huge and white."

"Got it." I give a thumbs-up. "Though I think we'll manage without you for a few days."

He grins and ducks through the gate. "Have fun cleaning!"

Eli waves back. "Good luck, Wi-Fi Man."

We turn to the task at hand, and it actually feels a little odd without Kenny. Wonder Dog has a seat in the grass to pant and watch. Eli brings a big bucket of water and adds in soap. We each take a scrub brush and kneel in the dirt along the patio. Before I begin, my phone buzzes in my pocket. I pull it out.

A text from Aunt Lexie pops up on the screen.

Aunt Lexie 1:42 p.m.

> Hey, Girl Reporter. How'd you feel about going to the Newseum tomorrow? I'll take the day off. Seems like you could use something fun this week.

I can't help smiling as I type back:

1:42 p.m.

> YES PLEASE.

"What is it?" Eli asks, watching me.

"My aunt is going to take me to the Newseum tomorrow."

"Museum?"

"*New*seum. It's a museum in Washington, DC, that's about the history of journalism and stuff. My parents promised to take me for my next birthday. We haven't gone yet because it's kind of expensive, and there's so many free museums in the city, and"—I lower my voice to mimic my dad—"'free is what America's all about!' He has a list of forty-seven places to go first, and we've only done nineteen. Which museums have you been to?"

"I've never been to DC, actually," Eli admits.

I stop cleaning to stare at him. "What? But you're only— fourteen miles away! And isn't your mom . . ."

"Yeah, I just never saw the point. I mean—I want to see my mom, but I never saw the point of Washington itself, really." He pours out some water to wash away the ash. "Your aunt seems neat, though."

He's clearly trying to change the subject, but I decide not to push it. "She is! But ugh, she's also being so annoying." I throw my hands up in frustration. "I'm trying to set her up with James—Mrs. B's grandson—but every time I get them in the same space, all she wants to do is talk to Mrs. B!"

Eli sits back on his heels and frowns. "Why would you do that?"

"Because he's clearly crazy crushing on her! Over the holiday, I tried to get her to admit it but she says"—I use air quotes to demonstrate my skepticism—"he's 'a wedding photographer' and she's 'just not that interested in wedding photography' and Mrs. B 'shares' some of Aunt Lexie's 'interests.'"

"I 'think'"—Eli uses air quotes back at me—"you might 'need' to use more 'air quotes' so I can fully 'understand' the situation."

I bump the back of his head with my hand. "*I* think you need to take this situation seriously."

Eli smiles, ducking. "Well, isn't it obvious? He's not just a wedding photographer. Get him to talk about the other stuff."

"What other stuff?"

"His travels. You know? The—what's it called?—human work? Humanity work?"

I sit up straighter. "Humanitarian work?"

"Yes, that one."

Humanitarian work means work that helps other people, normally people in desperate need—Aunt Lexie has explained that to me before. "What does James have to do with humanitarian work?"

"He does wedding photography to make money," Eli tells me. "But he uses the money to go on all these trips around the world with medical teams or something, to do photography for them."

My mind is whirling with possibility. "How do you know that?"

Eli shrugs. "I've overheard him on the phone in the backyard. Sometimes he complains to one of his friends about the weird wedding stuff people have had him do. Did he tell you about the time they released real doves at the end of the ceremony? It's hilarious. And most of the time he ends up mentioning his next trip. I think he's going to . . .

Nicaragua? Sometimes he even speaks a different language on his calls."

Eli might not be able to fly or disappear into thin air, but I bet his under-the-radar invisibility means he knows everything that goes on in this neighborhood. He's a reporter's dream source.

"This is perfect," I whisper, so excited I can barely breathe. "My aunt loves that kind of thing. Now I just need to get them both together . . ."

Eli scrubs a particularly tough black spot. "Could you get him to go with you to the Newseum?"

My eyes widen. "You. Are. A. Genius."

Smiling at the ground, Eli shrugs. Then, like a switch being turned, he suddenly freezes. Head cocked. Listening.

I frown. "What . . . ?"

Nothing sounds unusual. But then I notice the birds have stopped singing. And a car brakes with a soft groan somewhere not too far away. Wonder Dog hops up to bark, but Eli grabs her and closes her mouth with his hands.

"You need to leave," he whispers to me. "Now!"

All I manage to say is, "Huh?"

"Get her leash. You need to go. Don't make any noise."

There's something in his voice that makes my questions stick to my tongue. So I hook on Wonder's leash. Eli doesn't let go of her snout. He's not holding it tight, but she wiggles, wanting to go investigate the noises as a car door slams.

"Keep her quiet," he says to me. He gets to his feet and hurries across the patio. "Come on."

I pick up Wonder—she's almost too big for me, but it's easier to move like this—hold her mouth shut, and follow him. Wonder makes little *woof* noises, ears perked up.

Eli opens the gate and looks outside, then practically pushes me through. "Don't go straight to the street," he says. "Go through Mrs. B's yard or something."

"Okay. Are—"

But before I can ask anything, he closes the gate—quickly but silently—and vanishes. I blink, then let Wonder jump down as I edge into Mrs. B's yard. I glance back at Eli's house, trying to figure out what had him so spooked, but the only thing I see is Candace walking to the front door.

Chapter 15

MUSEUM TRIP EXPOSES MODERN MYTHS

Mom and Dad try to talk to me again, but I just hide in my room. There are three big things I need to think about. I write them down in my notepad, for record-keeping purposes:

The livestream. It's not that I'm upset about the baby. It's not even really that Mom did a livestream with me. The bit that feels lodged in my throat is the moment I turned to Mom, excited, and looked right in the eye of the camera. *That* moment tastes like betrayal.

The baby. I've pretty much decided the baby's name should be Lucy. Lucy Lane in the comics has a *lot* of different versions, and some aren't great, but when she's done right she is Lois Lane's best friend. *And* sometimes she has her own superpowers, and flies around as Superwoman. Perfect for my little sister.

Eli. This is the biggest puzzle to think about. Why was he so spooked? Even the first time Kenny came by, Eli didn't freak out that much.

By Tuesday morning, I've made a plan for the day with my parents using as few words as possible. But words of any sort mean, technically, I'm talking to them again. I guess.

I am very ready to get out—and, with any luck, finally force Aunt Lexie to actually spend time with James.

I push away thoughts of the three big things while I get dressed. Today I'm in a long red T-shirt and newspaper leggings. *What's white, black, and red all over? Nadia. On the job.*

Right around noon, Aunt Lexie pulls into the driveway and waves. I'm all ready and watching through the window. Over my shoulder, I call to Mom, "She's here!"

"Have fun!" Mom calls back. "I'll see you for dinner."

I run to the car without answering. Mom, Dad, Aunt Lexie, and I will meet in Arlington around five. That way, Aunt Lexie doesn't have to take me all the way back here. This sounds suspiciously like a setup for a family meeting about babies and blogs, but I'm not going to worry about that until *after*. Until then, I will have a perfect day.

"Hi, Girl Reporter," Aunt Lexie says as I slide into the passenger seat and buckle up. "How are you doing?"

"Fine." I pull my backpack on my lap and wrap my arms around it, unable to help jiggling my legs.

Aunt Lexie puts the car in reverse and backs out of the driveway. "Good. Your mom's kind of worried about you."

I make a face. Aunt Lexie smiles.

"Between you and me," she whispers, "I thought the livestream was a pretty bad idea, too. If she'd told me about it beforehand, I would have sent you a warning."

"Did you know she was pregnant?" I ask, remembering Aunt Lexie's comment on the bike trail.

Aunt Lexie hesitates, but nods. "She told me. But I promised I wouldn't tell anyone else. Your mom has had . . . some trouble with pregnancies in the past. She wanted to make sure everything was okay before she let anyone but your dad and me know." Aunt Lexie glances at me. "I knew you could handle it, but there's not a whole lot you can do when your big sister swears you to secrecy."

"I'll have to remember that," I say, shooting Aunt Lexie a smile. "I think it might be fun to be a big sister."

"Well, it always seemed a lot more fun than being the little one." Aunt Lexie winks, then passes me her phone. "You pick the music. Something to get us in a reporter mood."

We're pulling around the far side of the street now, and a brand-new birdhouse in Mrs. B's yard comes into view. She's standing in front of it, a hand over her mouth, staring. I can't help the wide grin that stretches across my face. Eli did it.

As we drive past, I raise my hand to wave. Mrs. B waves back, teary-eyed, and turns again to the house. I relax in my seat, letting a warm glow spread from my chest to my fingertips. Perfect day off to a perfect start.

The drive goes smoothly, pretty traffic-free. Out the window, I watch as the Mount Vernon Trail weaves in and out of view along the Potomac. Then we crawl through a million traffic lights in Alexandria. Then some more trail-Potomac views, then the airport, then more trail-Potomac. We turn onto one of the big bridges and cross into the city.

Even though Mom and Dad get lost every time they try to drive around here, Aunt Lexie navigates the busy streets and wild drivers like a pro. Before long, we're parked, I have my notepad out, and we're walking up to the Newseum itself.

And, just as I planned it, out front stands James Wilson. He's reading the long row of newspapers from around the world displayed against the wall, all of them featuring today's headlines. He looks serious, hands in his pockets and a satchel over his shoulder.

Aunt Lexie pokes my arm. "Um. Nadia? What . . . ?"

"Hi, James!" I call, waving.

He glances up and smiles at us. "Hey there. Glad I'm not late."

"Hello," Aunt Lexie says warily.

"I told Mrs. B that I was coming here with you today," I explain to my aunt. "And she said James was in the city doing a shoot this morning and so I suggested he could come with us because she said he's been wanting to check out the museum's Pulitzer Prize photography exhibit and so I told her to tell him what time we'd be here."

Aunt Lexie blinks. "Oh."

"I hope that's all right," James says, looking less certain now. "I thought . . ."

"Oh, it's fine!" Aunt Lexie smiles, and if she still looks a little awkward, at least she also isn't just gaping at us both anymore. "Totally. Let's go in."

We have to pass through security, buy tickets, pick up a visitors' map, and then I'm finally in the museum of my dreams.

"Okay, where do we start?" Aunt Lexie asks, opening her map.

I can't stop looking around. This hall is *huge*. Inspirational music plays in the background, and news quotes flash across a big screen while a rolling feed of headlines scrolls along the walls. Everything is crisp and clean and modern. I could totally see Lois Lane striding around, taking charge.

A quote forms on the screen. *"There are three kinds of people who run toward disaster, not away: cops, firemen and reporters."* — *Rod Dreher, newspaper columnist.*

I flip open my notepad and write it down. That perfectly sums up the sort of Lois Lane reporting I want to do. Maybe I can use it in my Junior Journalists Contest entry, if I ever come up with a real story.

While I'm still copying the quote, the screen changes again. This time, it's a group of teenage protesters. The focus of the picture is a boy holding a sign with a half smile frozen on his face. He has dark hair and brown eyes and he looks just like Eli—he's even wearing a hoodie.

Except . . . this boy has clean clothes and straight shoulders and a confident, goofy tilt to his head.

I've never seen Eli look like that.

"Should we start with the Pulitzer exhibit, since you came for that?" Aunt Lexie asks James.

"No, that's fine." James points toward an escalator with a START HERE sign. "I think we're supposed to go from the top down."

Pulling myself out of my thoughts, I suggest, "Let's do the opposite. Down and then up!"

Aunt Lexie shrugs. "Suits me."

We take an elevator to the first floor and start at the Berlin Wall—a chunk of wall and a whole guard tower that's been brought over and rebuilt here. Then it's on to a 9/11 room, then an exhibit about civil rights, and another about the history of journalism. I scribble anything that sounds interesting into my notepad. Writing works as a good excuse to lag behind James and Aunt Lexie, so they're forced to talk to each other.

Sometimes I catch bits of their conversation.

Aunt Lexie: "What kind of photography do you like best?"

James: "Portrait photography, actually. Especially candid—unposed."

Aunt Lexie, joking: "I thought all wedding photography was posed."

James: "Ha! Not all of it. But actually, I prefer to do portraits in communities, especially abroad—I like the challenge of capturing different people in different cultures, recording their lifestyles, that sort of thing."

Aunt Lexie, interested: "Oh!"

Then, later.

Aunt Lexie: "What was one of your favorite trips?"

James, not hesitating: "I went with Doctors Without Borders on a medical trip to the Dadaab refugee camps in Kenya.

It was intense, but everyone involved—patients and staff—was absolutely amazing."

Aunt Lexie, *very* interested: "That sounds fascinating. When were you there?"

James: "Back a few years ago. There's actually a film out now—"

Aunt Lexie: "Yes! *Lives on Hold*. I've been wanting to see it."

James: "Right—me too. It's set during the time I was there."

But even while I revel in this gold mine of journalism and matchmaking, I'm thinking about Eli. Maybe it's his terrible haircut that makes him seem so different from that boy. Or maybe it's the faint, tiny lines between his eyebrows when he isn't smiling. Or maybe it's the deep, dark patches of skin under his eyes, even darker than my dad's (and my dad's have gotten a lot darker since he started work at the Pentagon).

Maybe it's that the boy on the screen looked assured. Safe. And yesterday, Eli . . .

Something about the scoop doesn't feel fun anymore. Something's changed.

The *something* sits heavy in my stomach, a weight that grows every time I hold still long enough to notice.

At last we get to the top floor, where a long balcony scattered with tourists promises a great look at the city. James grabs the glass door and holds it for us while Aunt Lexie and I step out.

"Nice!" James says, walking to the balcony rail and lifting his big fancy camera from his satchel. From here we can see straight down the street to the Capitol building. In the early-summer glow of the crazy blue sky, the Capitol seems impossibly white. It almost hurts to look at it directly.

Aunt Lexie shades her eyes. "That's what I call a view."

James lowers his camera and glances across the balcony. "You know—I might head back to the Pulitzer Prize photography exhibit. I'll probably take a while to get through it, and I don't want to hold you two up."

"Sounds good." Aunt Lexie smiles at him. "See you in a few minutes."

James grins and goes inside. I lift my eyebrows at my aunt.

"Oh, shush." She swats my shoulder and heads toward the long line of information plaques along the edge of the balcony.

I follow her, tapping on my camera app to take some pictures of the street. Without James and his professional camera, it feels less silly to use my phone.

After a few minutes, Aunt Lexie makes a soft humming noise. "Hmm."

"What?" I look down at the plaque that Aunt Lexie is reading. It's a timeline of Pennsylvania Avenue.

"This street has seen a lot of history." Aunt Lexie points to the bold, big title, then trails her finger down to the spot right in front of her.

Above a small black-and-white picture, the caption reads: *Slave Pens on the Avenue. The Saint Charles Hotel at Third Street and Pennsylvania Avenue had below-ground pens where slaves were held while their owners stayed at the hotel.*

"Wow," I whisper. The old photo beside the text shows dark brick and ironwork, with a black doorway to the left. It's all under street level.

"Awful to think this was so close to our Capitol, huh?" Aunt Lexie says. "Literally only a few blocks away."

"Yeah." The grimy, dark photo seems to suck the warmth out of the bright summer day. I rub a sudden chill off my arms. "I'm glad slavery is over."

Aunt Lexie looks at me, surprised.

"I mean—I guess it probably still happens in some parts of the world . . ." I trail off as Aunt Lexie watches me with an expression I can't quite read.

I shrug, but that heavy something in my stomach suddenly grows ten times bigger. My scoop senses are going off, and I know, without Aunt Lexie saying anything, that I don't have the full story.

"Nadia," Aunt Lexie says softly. "I thought . . ." She pauses and drums her fingers on the sign, exhaling. "Do you know what I do at my job?"

I blink. "Traffic. What's that got to do with this?"

"I work in a law firm—right over there, actually." Aunt Lexie points toward the old Smithsonian Museum across the grassy mall. "We are committed to helping people who have been trafficked. That's the term we use for slavery now—human trafficking."

I can't help staring at her, my face heating. All this time, I thought she worked on *street* traffic. Like cars and trucks. But this is completely different.

"Human trafficking means that people are threatened, coerced, or sold for someone else's gain." Aunt Lexie meets my eyes, serious. "It happens all around the world, every day. Even here. It's just—hard to see."

"Hard to see?" I echo, my thoughts foggy and my voice faint.

Aunt Lexie nods. "In some ways, it's almost invisible."

Chapter 16

KRYPTONITE AND OTHER WAYS TO KILL A SUPERHERO

Invisible.

Eli.

I want to sink through the ground. My thoughts twist and tangle, and I don't know what to say or think or feel. It doesn't seem possible. It shouldn't be possible. And especially not here, not in the US.

Not Eli.

"But—how—why would anyone have a slave?" I stutter.

"Some people sell others online." Aunt Lexie stiffens, her gaze going distant, like she's thinking about things she won't say. Then she focuses on me again. "People can be . . . really terrible. Especially to kids. And there are other ways.

Sometimes it looks like historical slavery, where a person serves someone else in their house—we call them domestic servants. Some victims work on farms, or in restaurants, or hotels. Some are young, some are old—some foreign, some American. It doesn't look any one way."

A cold, sharp sting itches in my throat. "How do you know when you see it?"

"There are a few common signs." Aunt Lexie guides me away from the timeline plaques, to make room for other visitors. "Victims are isolated—especially from outsiders—so they don't have contact with anyone who might help."

Eli never leaves his yard.

"They are not well taken care of, generally—it's cheaper to replace a person than it is to pay doctor bills."

Eli always looks shabby.

"If the victims are foreigners, their passports and visas will be taken from them. Children don't go to school."

Eli doesn't go to school. He said he was homeschooled, but he always talked about classes like they happened in the past—like he doesn't do any of that now.

"Victims work without pay, or with so little they can't support themselves. Sometimes traffickers will hold a debt over their heads, or coerce them through threats and promises. Some traffickers control victims with drugs—illegal drugs, often, but sometimes drugs they need to stay alive, like in-sulin." Aunt Lexie shakes her head. "It's all complicated, and difficult."

A muffled haze settles around me. My chest hurts, a long, low hurt that doesn't start or end but just goes and goes. *It isn't right*, I think, *isn't right, isn't right*. My hands shake and clench, wanting something to grab, but my heart keeps skidding further and further into a world I don't understand.

Eli was supposed to be a superhero. Not this.

My eyes find the Capitol, white and blazing under the summer sky. It's so beautiful, and what Aunt Lexie describes is so ugly. The contradiction snags in my chest, a hook lodged deep.

Eli is always working. Every time I see him, he's working.

His clothes are torn and old.

He wasn't at the party. He's not supposed to meet anyone.

"You okay?" Aunt Lexie asks.

I nod automatically. I need to think. I need to talk to him. Get him to tell me the truth.

Aunt Lexie rubs my shoulder. "This has been heavy. Let's finish up and head out to meet your parents, yeah?"

I move with her. My gaze slides over pictures of parades, marketplaces, holidays. Tourists take selfies, and on the street below someone's playing a flute. The sky continues blue and brilliant.

How could I even wonder whether Eli is a slave? It's impossible. Even if slavery still exists, it wouldn't be on my street. Only a few miles from the capital of the United States! And it wouldn't happen to my friend. We're nearly the same age—he's just a little older. He's a normal boy.

But he's not, whispers a quiet part of me. *He's not normal.*

I catch Aunt Lexie's hand. My voice sounds hoarse. "I have a stomachache. Can I just go home?"

She looks worried and settles her arm around me. "Of course. Let me call your mom to let her know. Then we can get James."

I nod. This new information hurts my head, clenches my chest, squeezes my lungs. Memories and images overlap, crowding my thoughts. It's like a scene in *Man of Steel* when Superman doesn't know how to control his powers yet so he sees and hears everything and there's so much going on and—

Slavery. Everywhere.

Make it small, I think, reciting the line Ma Kent used to calm Clark in the scene. *Hold it in your hands. Focus.*

Everywhere.

Make it small.

In the United States.

Smaller.

In my neighborhood.

Smaller.

Eli.

The pressure eases. Eli.

The paralysis changes. Eli.

My whole body starts to shake. But I'm not afraid.

I'm determined.

Aunt Lexie's on the phone with my mom. I stop beside her. Numbness turning to fire, my fingers open my notepad. I stare at the page where I had been writing about walls torn down and journalists running into disaster.

In dark, firm letters, I write:

Is Eli a slave?

Aunt Lexie and James wait with me outside the Newseum. Mom picks me up, and Aunt Lexie goes back in with him, saying something about wanting to see the exhibit we'd missed. I can hardly concentrate. I can't talk. Over and over, while Mom and I drive home, the question repeats in my head: *Is Eli a slave? Is Eli a slave? Is Eli a slave?* It clamps my mouth shut, fills my brain. I need to know. I need to see him.

By the time we pull into the driveway, I can barely sit still. I need to take my questions straight to the source: Eli. And I want him, and only him, to tell me what to do about it.

"You've been really quiet," Mom says, parking the car. She casts me a concerned look. "Did you not like the Newseum?"

"It was great!" I unbuckle my seat belt and bolt from the car. "I'm taking Wonder Dog for a walk!"

I grab Wonder and her leash and sprint back down the driveway before Mom even reaches the front door. She was reading something on her phone, but she catches my arm. "Hold up. I thought you weren't feeling well."

"I'm fine. I—uh—I just wanted Aunt Lexie to hang out with James."

Mom smiles faintly. "Funny you should say that. Just have a look at all these texts I got during our drive."

She passes her phone to me, and my gaze skims over the screen.

Lexie 3:45 p.m.

> Hope Nadia is feeling better. Can you let me know if she is okay?

3:50 p.m.

Karen. Elizabeth. Quick. I don't know how your daughter managed it, but apparently I am going to a movie with James now.

3:52 p.m.

What has she done to me???

3:53 p.m.

And I've agreed to dinner afterward? What is happening???

3:53 p.m.

Also you should be happy because Mrs. Barton will be no part of this evening— apparently she is out of town doing some apartment shopping with James's mom.

3:54 p.m.

(Yes I know that because I tried suggesting we have dinner with his grandma so this wouldn't be a date.)

> Okay at the movie theater now. Must silence phone and be a proper adult. I will have my revenge on all of you yet.

Mom grins at me. "Good work, Nadia."

I force a smile and hand the phone back. "See? Everything's fine. I just want to go on a walk now."

"Well . . ." Mom tilts her head. "Okay. I need to order pizza or we'll be eating leftovers . . . But don't stay out too long. Maybe after dinner, we can talk about the blog and the ba—"

I cut her off. "Yep. Be back in a bit."

Wonder Dog and I hurry to the street, and I turn to the right, toward Eli's house. I'm still not exactly sure what I think is going on—*slave slave slave* thrums through my head—but I have to see him. Now.

The sun is creeping closer to the treetops. It's way later than one thirty, and for all I know Candace might be home soon. If she's his "trafficker," like Aunt Lexie called those sorts of people, I don't know what she'll do—to him or me—if she finds us together. That must be why he freaked out yesterday. Swallowing, I quicken into a jog.

No car in the driveway. That's a good sign.

At the back gate, I cup my hands to my mouth. "Woo WOO ooo ooo ooo."

No response.

I look into the backyard, but it's empty. A cloud covers the sky. Without sunshine or the path lights on, the garden seems expectant. Ominous.

Coming around the side of the house, I try the signal again. "Woo WOO ooo ooo ooo."

I pace to the front, making the call over and over. Wonder Dog paws my leg, probably worried I've lost it. Somewhere, a window scrapes.

"Nadia," Eli hisses from behind the bushes. "What are you doing?"

I check the shrubs. Eli has opened one of the basement windows and is frowning—no, scowling—at me. Fast as I can, I squeeze between the wall and the bush and squat in front of him. Wonder Dog wags her tail and goes to give Eli a lick, but Eli moves out of reach. I use the chance to slither through the window.

"What are you—?" he gasps.

I land with a *thump* beside him on a table pushed against the wall. Wonder Dog crouches, sniffing the windowsill, checking to see if I want her to follow.

"You can't be in here!" Eli whisper-yells. His dark eyes dart toward the street. "You can't be around *at all*, but you defi-nitely can't be *here*."

"I know—I know it's against the rules." Standing on the table, I study him close, *really* close. A lean, odd shallowness casts shadows under his cheeks, and in the dim light the skin under his eyes has colored from purple almost to black. His hair lies in its usual haphazard cut, but now that I'm really looking, I can tell it's dirty, wet-looking, flecked with dan-druff and dust. His clothes are the same I saw him wearing yesterday—no, they're the same he *always* wears.

All this time, he wasn't invisible because of some super-power. He's been invisible because *I* couldn't—*wouldn't* see the truth.

But hiding from the truth isn't what a journalist does. It's not what Lois Lane would do.

It's not what I want to do.

"Nadia," Eli prompts impatiently, glancing past the bush toward the road again. "I don't have time to talk."

"Are you a slave?" I blurt. "A—trafficked person?"

He turns and stares. My face heats, but my body stays cold. Wonder Dog leans through the open window and nudges Eli's head with her nose.

"No." Eli says it like I've gone mad, like he's talking to

someone who thinks the earth is flat or Lex Luthor is Superman. "There aren't slaves anymore. Not here."

I can't stop now. "*Do* you actually do school?"

He frowns. "I don't have time."

"Does Candace pay you for your work?"

"No. Why would she?" He crosses his arms. In his old T-shirt—without the hoodie—I can see the circle scars below his wrist gleam faintly. There are a few more up his arm, where they would normally be hidden. "It doesn't matter."

"Where do you sleep?" I look around the basement for the first time, realizing I haven't actually seen it since the botched party investigation. The big room is bare concrete, with storage boxes and spare furniture pushed out of the way. Before, I thought maybe this was his room—but there's nothing to sleep on. There's a small camera in one corner of the ceiling—the sort of security camera you might find in an old mall or something. A red dot blinks next to the lens.

I push back against the wall.

"It can't see you right here," Eli says. "And the audio quit working about a week ago."

"Why—?" I start to ask as I trace its angle to the other wall. There's a door left about two feet open. I lean to get a better view of the room beyond—except, there isn't a room. It's a closet. Maybe, *barely* big enough for a kid Eli's size to lie down in. A sleeping bag sprawls on top of lumpy pillows.

My heart thumps in my chest. "You sleep in *that*?"

Eli jumps off the table and pushes the door shut. With his back to the camera, he says in a voice as calm as a weather announcement, "I'm here because I *decided* to stay. And *you* need to leave."

I have to know the truth. Even if Eli doesn't want me to. Even if Eli doesn't know it himself. "Is Candace actually your aunt? How did you end up here?"

Eli moves back to the table—out of the camera's view—and rakes his fingers through his hair. We're eye to eye now—or, my eyes to his chin—but he still won't meet my gaze. "It isn't important."

"Of course it is!" My voice explodes out of me. "None of this is normal!"

"It's *safe*," he hisses. "I'm lucky, okay? Candace is predictable. There's a certain way things work. Everything has a pattern. Everything's under control."

"Including you."

"That's not the point," he snaps.

I hurry on, hardly knowing what words I'm going to use

but unable to hold them in. "My aunt said that human traffickers isolate their victims."

"I'm not a vic—"

"Is that why you never go out front? Unless someone's in danger and you can help. You're always—"

"That doesn't have—"

"—in the backyard." A new thought pops into my head. "And the party! During the party, you were down here, in *that*, when I was—"

"I only—"

"—looking for you. Are you even *allowed* to be seen? My aunt said traffickers don't take care—"

"Your aunt—"

"—of their victims and they keep kids from going to school and they threaten people with debts to keep them obedient. What will happen if—"

"*Stop!*" Eli grabs my shoulders and shouts in my face. "She'll send me back to *him*, okay?"

The questions clog in my throat. I stare at him—at his face, angry and fierce. His fingers pinch and his grip hurts. A wild pain lurks in his eyes.

I open my mouth.

"Don't ask who. Don't ask *anything*." Eli takes a shaky

breath. His grip loosens and his eyes go dull. All the life drains out of his voice. "Candace takes care of me, all right? I'm here because I want to be here. Because I haven't found anything better."

"Better?" The word comes out in a trembling breath.

He drops his arms and steps back. "Maybe I'll leave someday. Okay? When I know I can without Candace involving—him. But until then, *I* make the decisions. *I* know how to survive."

My heart starts to beat again. Harder and harder. "You can come to my house. Stay with us!"

Eli shakes his head, hopping down to the floor. "I'm not running. Not yet."

"Why *not*?" I demand, reaching through the window to grip Wonder Dog's harness. "It doesn't have to be like this. It *shouldn't*. You should be free."

A car rumbles down the street. We both stiffen. But it continues past the house. Not Candace.

"I am free," Eli whispers. "I'm not losing this, too."

I want to grab him. Drag him out of the basement. I want to make him see himself, ragged and drooping with his hands limp at his sides. I want to show him his own smile, the one that flashes all at once and turns him into an entirely different boy.

"Leave," Eli says. "Now."

"You saved Wonder Dog, and me." I lift my chin. "I won't give up on you."

He says nothing.

I crawl through the window again, nudge Wonder out of the way, and head toward the road. But this isn't a retreat. With every step, I'm thinking:

Journalists don't run from disaster. They run toward it.

Chapter 17

AUTHORITIES ARRIVE ON SCENE

I walk Wonder Dog home and slip her inside without Mom noticing. Through the front window, I can see Mom sitting at her desk, typing on her computer. It's like nothing's changed. The world's turned inside out, but everyone is acting the same.

I made a promise to Eli not to tell anyone, but that was before I knew he was in danger. I have to do something and I need help.

I sit on the porch steps and pull out my phone, scrolling to Aunt Lexie's number. If anyone can fix this, she can.

It goes straight to voice mail.

Right. She's at a movie.

After I push the phone into my backpack, I rub my eyes with my palms. Eli is a slave.

I'm almost sure.

No, I correct myself, forcing my brain to stop making excuses before it can start. *He* is *a slave*.

I squeeze my arms and glance at the office window again. Mom's staring at the screen, reading something now. If I talk to her, what would happen? I know she'd be skeptical—Nadia and her big imagination—she probably wouldn't even believe me. Or, if she did, she might try to use this for her blog somehow. Livestream the dramatic reveal of her daughter's friend's secret identity. Either way, Mom would for sure be mad that I've been sneaking over to Eli's without permission, and probably embarrassed, too—like she was at the house party.

And Dad's not home. Even if he were here, he'd just talk to Mom about it, and then I'd be back where I started.

I look around the street. Who else? In her texts, Aunt Lexie said Mrs. B is gone. So I jog down to Kenny's house instead.

Lights shine from inside. I run up and poke the doorbell. A minute later, the door swings open, and Kenny's mom is there. She's dressed fancy and putting in earrings.

"Oh," she says, surprised. "Hello. I thought you were someone else."

"Um, hi." I shift from foot to foot. "Is—erm—Pa—Kenny here?"

She shakes her head, then pats her hair down. "He's with his dad for the night. Sorry."

"Oh. Right." That's why he had to leave yesterday. He's not supposed to be around again for a few days. "Um—thanks. Have a good evening."

I walk back out to the street but stop to let a car go by. It loops around the median and pulls into Eli's driveway. Candace gets out, on the phone with someone. I freeze, watching. The *clip-clip* of her heels seems to echo through the silence.

What would Lois Lane do?

She'd have her photographer-friend Jimmy Olsen activate his emergency signal watch and get Superman's attention. Or, without the watch, she'd throw herself off a building or something so Superman would have to show up. He'd swoop in and take Candace straight to jail, then say something kind and meaningful about the whole situation. And Lois Lane would write the story with a killer headline.

Reaching into my bag, I find my Lois Lane press pass and grip it in my hand. The hard plastic bites my palm, but it makes me feel prepared.

Like it or not, I'm pretty sure there aren't actually super-heroes in this dimension known as "the real world." And I am very, very much in the real world now.

But there are other types of heroes. And I know the number to call them.

911.

—————— //////////// ——————

Even though Mom might worry about where I've gone and Dad might get home before me, I don't go to my house. Still holding my press pass, I find a hidden spot near some trees at the edge of the median and lie on my stomach near the top of the ditch. The dark clouds have thickened and the neighborhood hovers in dim light.

I can see Eli's house, but I'm pretty sure no one can see me. Candace's silver car is still in the driveway. Lamps shine behind the curtained windows. With my notepad and pen in hand, I wait. A steady thrum builds in me, loud enough to drown out my pounding heart. Whatever happens next, I'm here to record it.

Five minutes pass.

I told the 911 operator that I thought my friend was a victim of human trafficking. She said she would send a dispatch.

Ten.

I described Eli and gave them his address. Maybe I should have said more. Maybe then they would hurry.

Fifteen.

Finally, a police cruiser rounds onto the street. I had expected screaming sirens and flashing lights, but the car is dark, quiet, leisurely. Nothing about it says, *Someone's in danger! The world's gone wrong!*

I chew my lip, watching while the car pulls to a stop in front of Candace's house. Two officers get out—one young, lanky, and dark-skinned; the other about my dad's age, with silver-flecked hair.

The older man goes up the walkway and rings the doorbell, and the younger one takes a look around while he follows. I crawl farther up the ditch's side on my elbows.

Candace opens the door. Her eyes widen, but she smiles. "Oh, hello! How can I help you?"

"Good evening, ma'am," the older officer says. Both he and the younger one show their badges. "I'm Officer Tom Harrison and this is Officer Jay Paul. We had a call about some suspicious activity. Do you have a boy in your care, and could we talk to him?"

"Of course, just a moment." Candace turns and calls in a sweet, relaxed voice, "Eli*jah*, you have some guests!"

For a few long minutes, nothing happens. I lean up on my

arms, craning to see around the officers' bodies and into the house. Eli emerges, slowly, without his hoodie. He's wearing jeans that aren't as torn up as his usual pair, brand-new looking tennis shoes, and a clean blue shirt with long sleeves. He tugs the cuff over his wrists, even though the air is warm and humid. He still looks shabby next to Candace—in her prim business clothes and perfect hair—but without his usual outfit, he might just pass for normal.

The older policeman—Officer Harrison—asks some questions, his voice lowered so I only catch a couple of words. Eli answers so quietly I can't hear anything at all.

Biting my lip, I crouch-run to the police cruiser and hide behind the back right tire. Balancing myself with my hands on the warm pavement, I lean around the bumper to get a better view.

"Would it be all right if Officer Paul talks to Eli alone for a moment?" Officer Harrison asks Candace. "I'd like to ask you a few questions inside and see your foster paperwork, if that's okay."

"Of course!" Candace flashes another bright smile. She pats Eli on the shoulder and steps back. Officer Harrison follows her while Officer Paul leads Eli to the front lawn. Eli hunches, his eyes fixed on the officer's shoes.

Officer Paul kneels so his face is lower than Eli's. His back is to me, but I have the perfect vantage point to see my friend.

"You won't get in trouble for talking to me," the policeman says, tilting his head. Eli's gaze slides away, almost as far as the cop car. I press back against the bumper. "What's your relationship to Ms. Goldenberry?"

"I live with her," Eli murmurs. "She's my foster mother."

"How long has she been fostering you?"

"Two years."

"Do you know where your parents are?"

"No, sir."

"Where do you go to school?"

"I'm homeschooled."

I glare daggers at Eli from my hiding place.

Officer Paul shifts his weight. "Does Ms. Goldenberry have you do any work for her? Anything that takes a while, perhaps?"

Eli shakes his head, the filthy liar. All this time, he hasn't looked up from past knee-height. Officer Paul rubs his chin, like he isn't convinced.

"Has Ms. Goldenberry ever hurt you?" he asks.

"No, sir."

"And she feeds you well?"

"Yes, sir."

Eli's new shirt is almost baggy enough to make that plausible. It doesn't hang off his bones like the other one. Without even looking down at my notepad, I scribble, *TELL THE TRUTH*. As if he can read it.

Officer Harrison comes out of the house with Candace. "Everything looks good to me, Jay."

This is Eli's chance—a chance for justice to take down the bad guys. For the hero to save the day. Save himself.

But Eli's not acting like a superhero at all. He's acting scared.

"Well . . ." Officer Paul gets to his feet and tugs his shirt straight. "Thank you for your time."

Eli doesn't make a move to stop them. Candace settles her arm around his shoulders and gives him a little squeeze. Panic hitches up my throat like a gag. The police officers start to walk away from the door—toward the car, toward me. And Candace turns Eli around, guiding him back inside.

I scramble out from behind the car and shout, "Stop!"

Chapter 18

GIRL CRIES WOLF

The officers, Candace, and Eli all look at me, startled. Candace blinks. Eli gapes.

"Who are you?" Officer Harrison asks. "What are you doing here?"

My pulse pounds in my ears. I grip the press pass against my chest. "I'm the one who called 911. Eli shows plenty of signs that he's being human trafficked." I'm not sure if I've used the words right, but I plunge on. "You can't just leave him here!"

Officer Paul glances from me to Eli. Eli shuts his mouth and clenches his jaw. I can't tell if he's angry or afraid.

Officer Harrison repeats, "Who are you?"

"Nadia Quick," I answer, lifting my chin.

"She's my neighbor's daughter," Candace says. Her forehead creases with concern and she rubs Eli's shoulder. "I'm not sure—Nadia, why would you say this?" To the officers, she adds, "I didn't even realize they knew each other."

"Well, she knows his name," Officer Paul observes, giving me a nod of encouragement.

"I know Eli," I insist. "I know he's always in the garden and he doesn't do any schoolwork and he's not supposed to leave the yard."

"Oh dear. I can understand why you were worried, but I'm just not sure what to say." Candace looks down at Eli. She shouldn't be like this—she shouldn't be nice and polite and sweet, she should be raging. She should be spinning into her evil monologue, her master plan. Gently, she asks, "Eli, why would you tell her all that?"

Eli's gaze drops to the grass again. He mumbles, "We—we were just playing a game."

My breath catches. I can only stare.

"A game?" Candace repeats.

"We pretended we were superheroes." His voice is so quiet I almost can't hear over the pounding in my head. "We were making stuff up."

"*Eli*," I hiss. My throat is coated in sandpaper and my eyes burn. "Stop it! Tell them the truth!"

Eli shakes his head, just a tiny bit. He whispers, "It's not real, Nadia."

Pain flares through my chest. Like his words are a laser and it's carving a hole around my heart. The officers glance at each other with a look that says, *Someone's imagination is very active*. I've seen the look between my parents before. Candace just watches me with the same soft, kind expression. A hurricane of questions and doubts crowd my head. But I can't back down from the truth. I know the truth, *don't I*?

"Eli, you aren't safe here," I say, begging him. Maybe we were pretending other things, but the scars on his arms are real. The hollowness under his eyes is real. The brilliant smile that comes only when he's away from Candace is real. "Don't you want to leave?"

He stays completely still for a long moment, shoulders slumped, entire body curved in on itself. He doesn't even lift his eyes. His mouth forms the word, though he doesn't say it. *No.*

"I'm so sorry about this misunderstanding." Candace looks from the officers to me. "Are *you* okay, Nadia? Do your parents know where you are?"

I open and close my mouth. "I—I'm—"

"Thank you for your cooperation, ma'am," Officer Harrison says to Candace. "I think we can take it from here."

She nods. "Well, just let me know if you need anything else. Good night, Nadia."

I want to scream. I want to throw myself at Eli and grab his legs and pin him down. I want to give him a truth serum to force him to talk. I want Candace in handcuffs and a world with one less villain.

Instead, Candace and Eli go quietly inside. The door clicks shut behind them.

Officer Harrison stops in front of me on the way to his car. "Thank you for reporting your concerns," he says, though he doesn't sound particularly thankful. "But I think you should probably head home. It's about dinnertime."

"You can't just leave Eli," I plead, my voice quaking.

"He'll be fine, miss," Officer Harrison says. "I saw her paperwork. She's that boy's legal guardian, and everything looks normal. You don't need to be worried—there's nothing wrong here."

"But there is!" I can't get any air behind the words, and they come out ghostly and hoarse. "So much is wrong!"

Officer Harrison just shakes his head.

"Ease up a bit, Tom," Officer Paul says. He turns to me and his voice softens. "You live around here, right? How about I walk you home?"

I swallow. My body wants to sob, but I won't let it. I clench my jaw.

"*Do* your parents know where you are?" he asks, still kind.

"N-no," I admit in a whisper. "But—I live at the end of the street."

Officer Paul nods and steps onto the road. "I'd like to talk to them, I think."

Cold alarm shoots through my blood. "They won't help—they don't know anything."

More confused than accusing, Officer Harrison asks, "You called the police before you told your parents?"

I'm so frustrated—at them and Eli and myself—my voice locks up. I can't explain.

"I'll take you home." Officer Paul adds to his partner, "Be back in a few minutes."

Officer Harrison shrugs and slides into the driver's seat of their car. "Suit yourself."

Officer Paul follows me when I turn toward my house. I angle my head away to wipe the back of my hand over my cheeks, hoping he won't notice. This could be my last chance to prove to the police that Eli really is in danger, and I can't be crying like a little kid.

"I think you might be onto a lead here, Nadia," Officer Paul says quietly. "There's something . . . odd about this."

I whip my head around to stare at him. He smiles a little. He believes me.

Or at least, he's near to believing me.

"But we need more to go on," he adds. "At the moment, everything seems to check out. Eli's answers didn't necessarily raise any red flags, and I trust that Officer Harrison did a thorough examination of the files. If we can't find clearer indications of something wrong, we can't press an investigation."

"What can I do?" I ask, straightening. "What do you need?"

"Right now, why don't you just tell me more about Eli?" Officer Paul removes a small notepad from his back pocket. It looks a lot like mine. He asks me questions while we walk: How long have we been friends? What has Eli said about his circumstances? What is Eli doing when I visit? What were the games we played? What led me to believe he was being mistreated?

I tell him everything that pops into my head, especially about Eli gardening and the sleeping bag in the closet and the scars. When I tell him about our superhero game, the words taste bitter. I can't believe Eli would use it against me, use it to make me seem crazy. Confusion and hurt squeeze my ribs. But I talk until I run out of things to say.

"This is good to know." Officer Paul checks his notes and nods to himself. "We should be able to get a warrant at least. But in the meantime, you should keep your distance." He levels a serious look at me. "You are absolutely *not* to go after more evidence yourself, okay? Human trafficking cases can be dangerous. I'll come by during my rounds, check in on Eli. Maybe, when he trusts me, he'll open up."

I'm not totally sure Eli trusts *me*, and I'm not holding my breath that he'd get friendly with a cop anytime soon. But I keep that suspicion to myself.

"You did the right thing by calling us," Officer Paul goes on. "Even if it's just a hunch. But you should talk to your parents about it, too, you know?"

"Yeah," I admit. I rub my arms and stop at the end of my driveway. Maybe he has forgotten the part about talking to them himself. "Well, this is my house. Thank you for bringing me."

"No problem." Officer Paul turns onto the drive, and my heart sinks.

I drag my feet as I follow. The garage door is open, and Dad's bike is parked just inside, though I don't see him anywhere. I go through the front door, holding it for the cop. Wonder Dog comes bounding from another room, barking, and stops uncertainly when she sees the stranger. I kneel by her, wrapping my arms around her wiggly body.

Mom isn't in her office anymore, and dishes clink in the kitchen. The house smells like pizza. I clear my throat and call, "Mom? Dad?"

"Dia?" Dad comes into the foyer, already showered and changed. His eyebrows shoot up when he sees Officer Paul. "We—thought you were in your room. What's going on?"

Mom follows, and her eyes widen. "Nadia, are you okay?"

"Mr. Quick? Mrs. Quick?" Officer Paul holds out his hand to each of them in turn. "I'm Jay Paul. Nadia had some concerns about a house down the street, so I thought I'd bring her back after we assessed the situation. Can I ask you a few questions?"

"Of course," Mom says, shooting me a concerned look.

Dad touches Mom's arm. "We'll be happy to answer anything you want to know."

Officer Paul takes out his notepad. "Have you been to Candace Goldenberry's home at 9000 Stratford Lane?"

Mom blinks. "Uh—we were there for her house party recently."

"And did you meet a boy named Elijah? Goes by Eli?"

Mom shakes her head, glancing at Dad. "No—Nadia and another boy, Kenny, were the only kids there."

"Hmm." Officer Paul writes something down, then slips a business card out of his pocket and offers it to Dad. "Well, let me know if you notice any strange behavior at the house. If you see something that doesn't feel right, give me a call."

"Of course," Dad says. Mom nods.

"Have a good night, folks." Officer Paul tips his head to them, then glances at me. "And remember what we talked about. Don't go looking for evidence on your own."

I nod but don't know how to reply. Dad gets the door and the police officer leaves. When the latch clicks softly, both my parents turn to me. I squeeze Wonder tighter.

"Nadia, I . . ." Mom begins. "What . . . what is going on?"

I swallow. I've broken all my promises to Eli, anyway. I blurt out, "The boy who saved Wonder? He lives in Candace's basement. He's my friend. And Aunt Lexie told me about human trafficking—and I think he might be one of them. Trafficked."

"What?" Mom's eyes get big.

Dad frowns and squats in front of me. "Nadia, that's a pretty serious thing to say."

"This *is* serious."

"Isn't . . . this the boy you were investigating? The super-hero?" Mom asks, joining us on the floor. She searches my face. "I . . . didn't know you found him again. Why didn't you tell us?"

I grip Wonder so hard, she nudges my hand with a whine. "The—the story was ongoing then. And I promised him—but that's not important now."

Dad glances from Mom to me. "Okay . . . I want to get the timeline straight. When exactly did he go from being a super-hero to a trafficked kid?"

"I just—Today, I—"

They exchange a look. Like, *Aha, today she learned about human trafficking and immediately assumed her superhero is one of them.* A look like, *What are we going to do with this girl?* Like, *Well, she's finally lost it.*

"Don't you believe me?" I ask, my voice coming out in a whisper. The laser where Eli's words started carving out my heart returns, cutting its way toward a full circle.

"Nadia . . . You know your imagination is one of the things we love most about you." Dad brushes back one of my braids and Mom nods. "But to jump all the way to him basically being a slave? That's . . ." He glances at Mom. "I know today must have been pretty distressing, but . . ."

My body gets hotter and hotter the longer he talks. It's like they think I can't tell truth from fiction, like they think I've made all this up. When all the while, Eli is right down the street—and who knows what is happening? What if Candace is mad about the cops coming? What if she's hurting him, right now?

"This is real!" I insist. "Eli is in danger!"

Dad tilts his head. "Dia, simple logic would tell you he can't be a slave. If he was, why wouldn't he try to leave? Or—why wouldn't he have told the police?"

And I can't answer. Because I don't know the reason. I don't understand.

Mom rests a hand on her stomach for a moment. "Love, this has been a long day. Why don't we let it rest for now, and we can have a family meeting tomorrow? We'll talk through everything that's happened—the baby, this—and we'll see if there isn't something we can do. But for tonight, I think there's been enough excitement." She glances at Dad and he nods. "Let's just have dinner and watch a movie."

The laser finishes its circle, cutting my heart clean out. They don't believe me. They don't believe me.

Without a word, I grab Wonder Dog's harness and drag her with me up the stairs. Inside my room, I shut the door and sink down against it. Downstairs, my parents murmur together. Wonder Dog curls into a ball at my side.

They don't believe me.

Are they right?

Maybe I *don't* know the difference between real and imaginary.

Because if Eli *was* in trouble, why would he lie to the police? Why stay with Candace?

I flip open my notepad and push pages out of the way—*Is Eli a slave? TELL THE TRUTH*—until I find the next one. Blank, unmarked, waiting. I click my mechanical pencil and the lead comes out. The empty lines glow like the Bat-Signal—needing an answer, needing it now. I click my pencil two more times. Touch it to the paper, which wrinkles. I press hard, and the notepad starts to bend. Harder. The lead breaks through the thin paper with a *pop*.

I don't know how long I sit there. The sun sets behind storm clouds. It's well past dinnertime, but I don't feel hungry. I don't turn on a light. My parents' voices mumble downstairs, then I hear them going to their room. My head nods. I close my eyes. Just for a few minutes. Wonder Dog woof-snores.

An eerie sound breaks the quiet.

I lift my head off my arms, blinking away sleep. Listening.

Woo WOO ooo ooo ooo.

A mourning dove.

Eli.

Chapter 19

AREA WOMAN HUNTS HEROES

Eli?" I whisper-yell. "Where are you?"

I'm standing in the driveway, with Wonder Dog beside me. We stare into the darkness. Eli appears—seemingly from nothing—right in front of me. I jump and clamp a hand over my mouth to muffle a surprised cry.

Wonder, apparently expecting him, goes to sniff Eli's knee.

"What's going—?" I start to ask. But then the security motion-sensor light over our garage clicks on, and I get a look at him. My blood freezes.

A dark bruise runs the length of his right cheek. A split cuts down his lip, not even scabbed over yet. Before I can see more, he tugs his hoodie up and backs away from the sensor. A long moment passes. The light switches off again.

My voice trembles. "Eli?"

"I—I need to find my mom," he says. "She has a purple town house in DC. Which way is DC?"

I blink, my eyes adjusting again. "You can't just—go through all of Washington DC looking for a purple house. I mean, do you even know her address?"

Eli shakes his head quickly. "No, but I've been planning for a while. I needed to save up enough supplies." He unzips his hoodie pockets and shows me a collection of protein bars and other things I can't make out. Wonder gives that a sniff, too. "I didn't want to leave Candace until I was ready but she—she's gotten unpredictable."

"I—" My brain rushes through options. I could take him inside right now, but there's no way to guess how my parents would react. How do I know they'll believe him, or me? They could even give Eli back to Candace, thinking that would be the safest option. I can't trust they'll make the right decision.

Then there's the police—but I don't have Officer Paul's business card, and he's the only one who might give us a chance. Officer Harrison had an opportunity to protect Eli, and he didn't take it. Now Eli's hurt.

"Please," Eli says, his voice earnest even though his face is hidden. "I need to find my mom."

"Does—does Candace know you left?"

"I locked her in the closet. But she'll get out soon. Probably." The shadow where Eli stands sways a little. I reach over to steady him. He's shaking, even though his voice is steady. "I need to go now. How do I get to DC?"

"Aunt Lexie would know what to do," I say, thinking out loud. "She's a lawyer, and she works with kids like you. She'd believe us—she'd help. My phone's on my bed upstairs. I could call her and she'd drive us to DC. Then—then it would be faster to find your mom, and we could tell her everything."

"No, no. No one else." His voice falters. "I need to find my mom."

It's like he can only think one thing, say one thing. He's shaking worse and worse under my hand. Wonder Dog sits down beside Eli's leg and leans against him.

"If Candace tries to catch you, we need my aunt on our side." I shift away, glancing up at my bedroom window. "I'll just grab my phone and—"

"*No.*" He draws a sharp breath and backs down the driveway. "If you're going to break your promise again—"

"Wait!" I grab the sleeve of his hoodie to stop him from leaving. Invisibility superpowers or not, I know he can vanish. And if he does, I'll lose him forever. "I'm sorry. I won't tell my aunt. I won't tell anyone. Just let me help."

Eli doesn't move. Doesn't seem to inhale. But his shaking stops.

"Okay," he agrees at last. "How do I get to DC?"

I bite my lip. The city is huge, and there must be about a million town houses. If we were superheroes, it'd be the work of a few minutes. As kids, I have no idea how to pull it off. But that doesn't matter right now. I tried to help Eli my way, and now he's worse off than before. And I absolutely can't let him go alone.

"You can ride a bike, right?" I ask him. "For a few hours?"

Eli nods slowly. "I think so."

"Okay." I stand straighter. "I can get you to DC."

"You're coming?" he asks. I can't see his face. I can't tell if he sounds hopeful or nervous.

"Absolutely. Heroes don't let heroes fight alone." I nudge Wonder Dog over to him. I'm not totally positive Eli won't just bolt if I leave him alone. "Hold Wonder. I have to get the bikes and her leash and stuff."

Before he can say anything else, I take off down the driveway. Opening the main garage door would alert my parents that I'm outside. So I take the long way around, via the gate to the backyard.

At the other side of the house, I turn the knob on the

smaller garage door. Sure enough, it hasn't been locked for the night. I ease it open and step into the garage.

Everything's dark. I hesitate. The light switch is inside the house and Wonder Dog might bark if I turn it on and my parents might wake up and then Eli will definitely run. Not worth the risk. Junk and storage bins are stacked up on either side of me with a narrow path down the middle. We always keep our bikes near the front, which ordinarily makes sense, but as I creep through the stuff, trying not to knock anything over, I'm not sure I'll be able to fit them through this canyon.

I get around the mower and ease Mom's bike aside so I can get mine out. I have to angle the handlebars so they won't catch on each other. Walking backward and pulling the bike with me, I inch back the way I came. Everything's harder in the dark, but my eyes adjust to the faint streetlight coming in through the small windows.

Finally, I reach the door again. I pull my bike out onto the back patio and put the kickstand down. Then I run in for my dad's bike. Eli isn't as tall as him, but we can adjust the seat. While I'm there, I grab Wonder Dog's leash off Mom's bike and stuff it under my arm. At the last minute, I remember to get two helmets—I loop their straps around my other arm. Fully loaded with equipment, I again make the journey to the patio.

Dad's bike is harder to maneuver, and the pedals snag on a box.

I freeze, but all remains quiet inside the house.

Soon I tug Dad's bike out next to mine. I just need one more thing: water. If I've learned anything from our weekend outings, it's that you never go on a long ride without plenty of water.

One of my backpacks is hanging by the door to the basement. I pull it down, open the garage fridge, and stuff several water bottles inside. I slip my notepad in a secure pocket, too, and check to make sure I have some spare pens. Knowing the supplies are there calms a quivery, jittery part of me, and I can finally take a deep breath.

Sorry, I think to my parents. Then I take my bike's handlebar in one hand and Dad's in the other and—wobbly and slow—walk them around the side of the house, through the gate, and down the driveway.

"Eli?" I whisper.

And there he is, again, appearing out of nothing. Wonder Dog wags her tail at me but doesn't bark. Maybe she's catching on to the etiquette of espionage. In a few minutes, I've got Eli's seat adjusted, helmets on both of us, and Wonder Dog attached to my bike.

"We need to get to the Mount Vernon Trail," I say to Eli

as I kick off from the driveway. He follows my example, less steady on his bike. Wonder Dog trots at my side. "Technically no one's supposed to be on it after sunset. But I think it'll be okay."

"What if we're caught?" he asks, coming up beside me.

I shake my head. "The trail is near the road, but my family's driven down the parkway loads of times and you can't see the path—not with headlights on. We'll be fine."

I hope. I don't exactly have experience breaking the law for a noble cause. But it's also true that I've never seen anyone on the trail at night.

We cruise to the bottom of the long, easy hill and approach the first big road. I roll to a stop and lean out to check for traffic. During the day, it's always busy—commuters and visitors and tour buses—but right now it's almost abandoned.

Almost. A car approaches from the right, so I walk my bicycle back where the trees will hide us. Eli follows. Wonder Dog leans against my leg. My heart pounds harder than it has in my entire life as the car gets closer. Closer. If it turns onto our street, we're doomed.

This is nuts, I think. *We're going to get caught.*

Trying to swallow down the panic clawing at my throat, I whisper to Eli, "Hey, Eli, do you think you could use your invisibility? Keep us hidden?"

Eli glances at me without turning his head. After a moment, he answers, "Sure. Done."

The car goes past without turning. We're clear.

"Keep it up," I say, grinning at him with relief. I stand to use maximum speed while we cross the parkway. As soon as I'm over—Wonder next to me, Eli right behind—I shoot past the Riverside parking lot and turn left onto the trail. In moments, we're surrounded by trees.

My nerves buzz like I've got tiny sparks zinging through my skin. My fingers tingle and my heartbeat keeps going superfast. Though ordinarily I'd be in bed by now, I'm nowhere near tired. I could bike all night long and still be alert.

I've done this trail before, but normally I have the whole day to cover the fourteen miles between us and the city. It's not going to be easy getting there like this, at night, with possibly Candace or my parents trying to find us.

"We need to conserve our energy," I say to Eli when he catches up. I force myself to pedal slower. "It's a long way to DC."

"Got it," he says. He already sounds almost out of breath.

We cross a wooden bridge, and the slats rumble under us. Eli swerves, unprepared.

"Careful!" I call.

He steadies the bike. We bump back onto the normal paved trail, and my legs settle into a rhythm. Eli stays beside me. I hear him take a deep, deep breath and exhale.

"How are you feeling?" I ask.

"Sort of . . . weird." He glances at me. "Not bad. Just . . . *weird*."

"Like, electric weird?"

He shakes his head. "Like . . . floating weird. Falling weird."

I take a mental note so I can add it to my record later. The moon flits in and out behind thick clouds, and as my eyes adjust, it becomes easier to see the smooth paved path between the trees. For a few minutes, the only noises are the *shhh shhh* of our wheels and gears, and the *thump-thump* of Wonder's paws, and the splashing of the Potomac River against rocks. My legs go up, down, up, down. My shoulders start to ache from the extra weight in my backpack.

"What's the first thing you'll do once—you know—you find your mom?" I ask Eli.

He's silent for a moment. "I'll go back to school."

I laugh. "You must really like school. I definitely would have put cookies or something at the top of my list."

"I do. Or, did. I'm good at following instructions. I always knew what I needed to do."

I nod, thoughtful. "I guess school is kind of safe, huh?"

"It was for me."

The Potomac, on our right, gleams. It smells like rotten trash. Moisture pricks along my exposed arms, the heaviness of a storm that's not quite here. If it could just hold off until we make it to DC, that would be awesome.

Cars pass on our left, their headlights flashing over the trees between us and them. For now, we're well hidden. The drivers zoom by, oblivious. I wonder where they're going and what they'll do when they arrive and whether anything exciting is happening to them. In their stories, Eli and I are just margin notes. Those drivers don't even know their lives have just brushed shoulders with ours.

Another headlight beam catches on the bushes ahead of Eli and me. But it stays there—it doesn't keep going. I stop pedaling and look over my shoulder.

A car is coming down the parkway, moving slow—really, really slow. Like it's looking for something.

I hit my brakes and hiss, "Eli! Stop!"

He obeys, shooting me a confused look. Then his eyes catch on the car, creeping closer.

"Hide," I whisper. For all I know, whoever's in there could be listening with their windows down. As quietly and quickly as possible, I lift my bike a few inches and step toward the river, away from the road, to add an extra layer of cover between us and the lights. Wonder Dog sticks close to me, though she tries to have a sniff at the leaves. Eli tugs his bike after us, and we both crouch, watching. I slip an arm around Wonder to hold her down.

The headlights grow clearer. They're a distinct circle shape. I don't know the model of the car, but I know those are unusual.

"It's Lady Liar," Eli murmurs.

"Who's that?" I ask.

"Candace. Lady Liar." He stares straight at the car. "Successful businesswoman and popular hostess by day, builder of underground operations at night."

I nod, catching on. "People are convinced she's the best thing since organic bath bombs, but we know her true identity. She's a supervillain."

"Don't worry. Invisibility is engaged at maximum."

Even so, I hold completely still, hardly breathing. The car inches by. It continues crawling along the road, brake lights flashing red every now and then. Finally, finally, it disappears into the distance.

I let out my breath. We have hours of biking ahead of us.

Some of it will be totally out in the open. All it will take is bad timing for us and great timing for Candace and we'll be sitting ducks.

A part of me doesn't want to leave this spot.

Eli stands, taking the handlebars of Dad's bike. "Ready?"

I look up at him. His expression is grim, determined. He's going with or without me.

"Yes." Checking to be sure there's absolutely, definitely no sign of Candace and her car, I pull my bike onto the path again. I lower my voice to a Wonder Woman-ish grown-up hero tone. "Come, Invisible Boy! *To Washington!*"

He swings his leg over the bar. "On your signal, Lightning Lane."

I grin and push off.

Right about then, the first raindrop hits my nose.

Chapter 20

LIGHTNING LANE VS. STORM

The single drop turns to a continuous downpour. It gets hard to see the path in front of us, and we have to move more carefully. Eli and I don't really talk—we're too focused on keeping our bikes steady. Wonder Dog doesn't have a problem with the water and keeps up without any sign that she's tired.

After what feels like hours, we hit the first long stretch of trail that runs right next to the road. No trees to conceal us. I slow and touch my foot to the ground, twisting to look at Eli. His soaked hair flops on his forehead. The cut is way more uneven than I noticed before.

"We need to watch for cars," I tell him, raising my voice against the pounding rain. I reach down to rub Wonder's ear. "If we see one, we should get on the side of the trail by the Potomac. There's not a whole lot to hide behind . . . but I think the curve of the hill will keep us out of view."

Eli nods. Water drips off his nose.

"Okay," I say, half to him and half to myself. I give Wonder Dog a pat on the head and face forward. The road and the long, unlit path stretch out in front of me, and—in the distance—the lights of Old Town Alexandria glimmer. "Okay. Here goes nothing."

I take the lead, pedaling into the wide open where anyone could see us. Even with the dark and the rain, I feel completely exposed. I'm not sure how late it is now, but we're definitely past the time where we could pretend to be stupid kids who didn't realize the trail was closed, who just wanted to do some innocent night biking, etc. If a cop patrols the parkway—and they do, sometimes—or a friendly driver spots us, we are in huge trouble.

And those are the best-case scenarios. If Candace catches us, what's going to happen?

I try to keep my imagination in check, but I have some very vivid ideas: She could chuck us in the Potomac. She could lock us in a closet forever. She could tie us to metro rails. She could . . .

"Nadia," Eli says behind me. "Slow down. I can't keep up."

"Oh." I check my pace and let my bike idle. Eli's almost ten feet back. "Sorry."

We continue to follow the trail. The town gets steadily closer.

Then, far away and on the other side of the street, headlights appear. A car. Coming this way.

"Take cover!" I call to Eli, slamming my brakes and throwing myself off my bike and dragging it (and Wonder Dog) behind a bushy, low-branched tree. Eli joins us a second later, breathing hard. Wonder licks rainwater off our faces while we both kneel. The car approaches, fast—this person is in a hurry to get somewhere.

The headlights are perfect circles. The same shape as Candace's.

The car zooms by, heading in the direction we came from. My stomach tightens.

"Lady Liar?" I ask Eli.

He shakes his head. He was crouching, but now he sits on the soggy ground. "I couldn't tell."

Wonder Dog climbs into Eli's lap, giving him curious sniffs. Since we've already stopped, I open my backpack.

Despite the rain, the inside seems pretty dry—though my soaked hands can't really feel the difference.

"Here." I pull out a water bottle and pass it to Eli. "We'll rest a few minutes."

He opens it while I get another one for myself. After a few sips, I pour the water into the tiny cap and let Wonder have a drink. As my heart slows to a normal pace, my body starts to ache. My leggings are soaked, my shirt is soaked, my braids are soaked, and the rain just keeps coming. It's the sort of rain that's somewhere between muggy-horrible and cold-horrible. I take another swallow of water and try to make my muscles relax.

Wonder lays her head on Eli's leg, and he absently rests a hand on her back. My gaze catches on his jeans—still the nice pair he wore when he talked to the cops. And he's wearing the like-new shoes, too.

"Where'd you get those clothes?" I ask.

"Candace had a rule." He tugs his sleeve. "If official people came by, she'd call me Eli*jah*. And I had to change into this special outfit. We practiced a few times. I got really fast at changing."

"Oh." Just the sort of scheming one might expect from a supervillain. "How did you end up with her, anyway? With Lady Liar, I mean."

Eli rubs Wonder Dog's ear between his fingers. Finally, he says, "My dad left me with her. I think he owed her money."

"Your dad *left* you?" I echo, staring.

"That was actually one of the nicest things he ever did." The corner of his mouth tilts, but not really in a smile. "Anyway. I was supposed to pay off the debt, but Candace said that keeping me cost more than I was helping her, so it just got bigger and bigger. I figured out a while ago that she wasn't ever going to let me leave."

"What about your mom?" I ask. "Why didn't she stop it?"

"She wasn't there." He shifts. "She got arrested when I was a kid, and the judge gave me to my dad. I didn't even know she was out until my dad handed me the photo with her at the town house, right before he dropped me off at Candace's. Candace said that if I behaved, she might give me to my mom instead of him. But I don't think she meant it."

"That's awful," I murmur. The words feel small, but I don't know what else there is to say. If that *was* Candace's car, where was she headed? And why was she going so fast?

We need to keep moving.

The rain lightens a bit, at last. I stand, brushing the mud and grass off my leggings, then pull my bike off the ground. Wonder hops up and resumes her place beside me.

Eli groans as he pushes himself to his feet. For a second, he presses his arm against his side. Then he gets his bike.

"How are you doing?" I watch the way he winces as he walks to the path.

"Fine," he says. "Just sore."

I nod. "Invisibility activated again?"

He gives me a weak salute. "All set."

We go on, and soon cross a bridge into Old Town. The brick town houses are golden and glowing in the misty rain. The normally busy streets are strangely quiet. When we pass a bank, the old-fashioned clock tower says 3:10. My eyelids get heavy, as if just knowing the time has made sleepiness catch up with me.

"We should go a block over," I tell Eli, rubbing my knuckle against my eye. "The main road cuts right through Alexandria, and there are bound to be cars."

"Okay."

I take us down a back street to South Saint Asaph. The sidewalk is paved with bricks and covered in random bumps and dips from tree roots. I slow to a crawl to keep from getting thrown off my bike. But it's better to be here than in the middle of the road, I figure, because at least the parallel parked cars give us some cover.

So far, though, the city sleeps.

Tree branches loom above us, and the town houses cluster together on both sides. Lanterns shine by people's front doors—some of them with lightbulbs, but others with real flames. It's like we've fallen back in time.

In the shadowy alleys and around closed shops, men lurk, sleeping. Homeless. I try to pedal extra quietly as we pass.

About halfway through the town, we come to a cobblestone cross street—one with fist-sized rocks instead of normal smooth asphalt. I dismount at the edge.

"It will be easier to walk here," I explain to Eli.

He mimics me. My feet slip and slide on the wet stones. Wonder Dog wobbles a bit herself, bumping into me. On the far side of the street, a man lies very still on top of a sleeping bag, with something small and fluffy curled against him. My heart beats faster. Off our bikes, we're easier to catch.

Eli suddenly pitches into me. We fall in a heap of kids, dog, and bicycles. My elbow collides with the sharp edge of a pedal and I yelp. Eli lands, more on the hard stones than the bikes, but he only grunts. Wonder Dog whimpers.

"Ouch," I whisper, easing myself up.

"You kids okay?"

I jump and nearly send myself sprawling again. The homeless guy is hurrying toward us. A scream pushes up in my throat and freezes there.

He picks up my bike. Wonder Dog keeps her distance, eyeing the stranger but not barking like she normally would. The homeless man takes Eli's arm to lift him to his feet. Eli gasps and clenches his jaw. The guy frowns.

"You hurt, son?" he asks, leaning to get a better look at Eli.

"I'm fine," Eli says a bit tonelessly.

I bite my lip.

The homeless man pushes up Eli's hoodie sleeve and moves his arm to catch some of the streetlight. Welts shine all the way from Eli's wrist to his elbow, glistening and new.

"You didn't tell me—" I start to say, hoarsely.

Eli watches the homeless man, but he doesn't jerk away.

"How's your other arm?" the man asks.

"She didn't get to my left."

"I have some first aid supplies," the man says to no one in particular. "We should clean this up."

He releases Eli and starts to walk away. This is our chance to escape. But instead of running, Eli follows him to his sleeping bag area. I wheel both our bikes over. The homeless man rummages in his stuff with one hand, then pulls out a small, slim red box.

A familiar red box.

When he turns around, I look again at the man's face and

I get my first clear view of him. Kind amber eyes smile back at me. I look at the fluffy white thing on his sleeping bag. The dog—Girl—whose nails I helped trim. She eyes Wonder Dog warily but doesn't get up from her tightly curled spot.

This is the man I met outside Synergy, while Mom did her interview.

He nods, like he sees I've finally recognized him, and shifts his attention back to Eli. "I don't know a whole lot," he mutters to himself, "but I know this."

Eli's eyes dart up to the veteran's. Then he asks, "What's your name?"

"Jim. Vet Jim." He opens the kit and fiddles around. I keep ahold of both our bikes, watching closely. Vet Jim puts the kit on the trunk of a nearby car and rips open some slim packages. The trees lean over us, holding off the rain.

"This will sting," he warns Eli. "But that's 'cause it's doing its job."

When he presses the small square wipes against the wounds, Eli sucks in a breath and holds it. But otherwise, he doesn't make a sound. Vet Jim works fast, flying through several wipes and then applying something shiny and wet over the welts. He presses on Band-Aids until Eli's arm is pretty much covered in them. All this time, he doesn't ask us any questions.

After the last Band-Aid is secure, Vet Jim pulls Eli's sleeve back down to his wrist. "Those should be changed in a few hours," he says. "Watch for fever or heat around the wounds. That could be a sign of infection. Do not pick at the scabs, even if they itch. If they turn a strange color or seem to be getting worse, call my office and make an appointment."

Eli glances from me to Vet Jim. "Um. Okay."

Vet Jim nods and snaps the first aid kit closed. Then he puts it next to his sleeping bag and sits down beside Girl, evidently ready to go back to bed.

I lean my bike against the nearby car and reach into my backpack. I set two of the unopened water bottles next to him on the ground.

"Thank you," I whisper.

"Thank you for your service," he murmurs, but I don't think he's talking to me.

I let Eli take Dad's bike, and we walk around Vet Jim's area until we're on the sidewalk again. We both mount and start off without saying anything. I look back halfway down the block. Vet Jim is sipping the water, one hand resting on his dog.

Even though our progress is slow, and even with our unplanned stop, we pass through Old Town sooner than I expected. Then it's onto East Abingdon Drive, which at least keeps us separated from the main road. Here, we don't need to duck for cover when the occasional headlight comes down the parkway. So far, none have been perfect-circle shaped.

The wind picks up, stabbing through my damp clothes. I shiver. The raindrops grow, big and fast. Far away, I think I hear thunder—or maybe a metro train.

Eli breathes hard behind me, in little pant-gasps. Wonder Dog huffs a little every few steps. My muscles hurt. I know we need to rest again. Soon.

The trail veers farther from the road as we near Ronald Reagan International Airport. The rain lashes at us now, and I almost can't see, even though bright lights surround the airport. We're about halfway to Washington, DC. I think. I don't have the heart to tell Eli we still have halfway to go. I'm not even sure *I* can make it the rest of the way.

Was it only this morning that Aunt Lexie was driving me down the parkway? Just twelve hours ago when I was at the Newseum with her and James?

I wonder how their date went.

"Think you could get us some better weather?" Eli calls over the rain.

I don't understand him the first time. "What?"

"Lightning Lane." I hear a smile in his voice. "Sounds like

you should have some weather powers, along with stopping time."

I snort. "You're the one who can fly. Why don't you just pop us over to DC?"

"Only if you want the government to shoot us down." He shakes his head, like a dog shaking off water. "Wi-Fi Man was right, even my invisibility won't help with that."

"Hmm."

Soon we're in Gravelly Point Park, and I slow, watching for a gap between the trees. When it comes, there's Washington, DC. The rain pauses, like a curtain drawn back, and the Washington Monument shines bright white against the velvety sky and the Jefferson Memorial glows at the Potomac's edge.

Without stopping, I point. "Look, Eli!"

Eli, beside me, lifts his head. He swerves, almost hitting Wonder Dog, and I yank on my brakes. He jerks in the other direction, over some wet leaves, and his bike skids sideways. The next thing I know, he's crumpled on the ground.

"Eli!" I hop off my bike, throw down the kickstand so it won't fall on Wonder, and hurry to him. "Are you okay?"

He slowly sits up, wincing. "Y-yeah."

But his nice jeans have ripped at the knee, and the skin beneath looks torn. I carefully pry away the edges of the fabric, and something sticky and warm coats my fingers. Bile rises in my throat. Straightening, I turn to the bike. It's fallen on its side, one wheel spinning.

The other wheel is bent and still.

Eli sees it, too. He tries to get to his feet, but I have to grab his arm and help.

The rain starts again.

"That bike's totaled," I whisper, my body heavy.

"I can walk," he says breathlessly. "We can keep going, right? We have to get to DC. I have to find my mom."

I look back across the Potomac, to the distant Washington Monument now cloaked in a blurry downpour. It looked so close a few minutes ago, but now it seems like it's never been farther away.

I tighten my hand on Eli's arm. "Yes. We walk."

Chapter 21

A NEW DAY IN WASHINGTON

By the time we make it to Arlington Memorial Bridge, Eli has stopped limping, but he stumbles with every other step. I keep one hand on his uninjured left arm and one on my bike's handlebars. We left Dad's bike on the trail—nothing we could do about it—but I want to keep mine. Partially so Wonder Dog still has something to be tied to. Partially because, if worse came to worst, I could put Eli on my bike and send him ahead. Like, if Candace caught us or something.

We stop under the bridge, right near the Potomac. Over our heads, cars hum across the water. It seems like there are more out now, but I can't tell if that's because it's getting closer to early commute time or if it's because this road is always busier than the parkway.

"Break?" I ask, almost too exhausted to speak.

Eli slumps against the curved bridge wall. He looks more tired than I feel, if that's possible. Wonder Dog flops down.

"We can rest for a few minutes," I say. "This should be safe."

He nods and slides to the ground, one arm pressed against his side. I let Wonder off her leash and she scoots over to rest against Eli's leg. They both close their eyes, and just like that they're out. Practically snoring.

I sit on the other side of Wonder and rest my hand on her back. The gentle rhythm of her breathing makes me sleepy. But I try to push that away and concentrate on our next hurdle: the bridge.

Bikers use the sidewalk on the bridge when they cross. But this is one place we'll have absolutely no cover. We won't be able to duck behind something or jump off the road—not unless we dive over the guardrails into the river.

I run my hand down Wonder's back. Once we're across the bridge, there's the teeny tiny problem of where in the huge city we're going to locate Eli's mom's town house. It would be easier to find Aunt Lexie's office. I don't know exactly where that is, but I know it's in the area of the original Smithsonian building. Though I'm not sure what the company is called . . .

I wish I had my phone. Then I could fix all of this in one conversation with my aunt.

The humming of the highway grows muffled and a layer of wool seems to separate me from the world. Like a phantom, half dream, I imagine Kenny standing in front of me. He holds out his Superman window stickers. *You like superheroes, right?*

I bolt up. My neck pinches, as if I've been asleep for a while. But my brain clears. I have it—I know how to cross the Potomac and get Eli to safety. I'm just . . . not so sure how Eli's going to take the suggestion.

"Ah!" I rub my eyes and pull myself to my feet. My legs creak in complaint. Wonder huffs a sigh and stands. I nudge Eli's foot. "We have to keep going, Eli. Come on."

He groans. "I don't know what I have left, Lightning Lane."

"Invisible Boy, you stop that right now." I put my hands on my hips. When I look past him at the area beyond our shelter, the rain has all but stopped. "Look, I even made the weather nice for you. So up—up!"

He mutters, but takes my hand when I offer it. I help set him upright. But as he straightens, he lets out a hiss and presses his arm to his side.

"What's wrong?" I ask.

"I'm not sure." Eli turns to catch more light from the

street. Then he rolls the hoodie and his T-shirt above his ribs. I lean over to get a look, too.

He's thinner than I thought, his bones pressing against skin like they're trying to get free. But that's not the worst of it. An angry bruise has formed from about his armpit down toward his waistband. It lumps up in places, and the color blends from dark to splotches of near black.

"Holy cow," I whisper.

Eli sighs and covers it again. "It'll be fine. I've had worse."

I stare at him. I wish he had let Vet Jim take a look at it—but a first aid kit probably wouldn't do much good here.

Determination settles in the pit of my stomach. It makes absolutely no sense to launch a citywide search for Eli's mom when he is this injured. I hook Wonder Dog's leash onto my bike and lead the way out from under the bridge onto the street. Instead of turning toward the Lincoln Memorial and DC, I push through one of the tall hedges at the side of the road and head toward Arlington.

"Where are you going?" Eli asks, his face pale. He looks back at the Lincoln Memorial. "DC is that way."

"I know, but we need to get some help."

Eli's eyes sharpen. "Help?"

"Look, Eli—I want to find your mom. And I know you don't want to tell anyone about this." I tighten my fingers around the handlebars and take a deep breath. "But we can't do it alone. We don't even know where to start. And you're hurt. Paddle—Wi-Fi Man is nearby. I find him, he can help us find my aunt, and she can help us find your mom."

Eli still stands there, arms loose, half turned toward the distant memorial. "I could go to DC now."

I see him wondering—almost like his thoughts are mine—whether he'd be able to find the purple town house by himself. Whether he needs me, now that he's this close.

"There's no place to hide over there," I point out. "If Candace comes, she'd catch us in a heartbeat. I mean, *anyone* crossing that bridge is going to see two soaking-wet kids and a dog walking suspiciously early in the morning." I nod toward the bushes. "We need to go this way."

"I need to get to my mom, Nadia," he says. "That's all that matters."

"I know," I agree. "And I know I promised, so if you say no, I won't do it. I trust you. I really, really, really honestly truly think this is the only way we're going to find her." I lift my chin and look him full in the face. Like always, his gaze lands somewhere around my shoulder. "Can *you* trust *me*?"

Eli shifts his weight, mouth twisted in thought. I hold my breath. My heart beats faster, and I wonder with a sudden ache—*can* he? Because no one else seems to. Not the police.

Not even my parents. And I don't know if that's their fault, or mine.

Then, slowly, Eli lifts his gaze. Meets my eyes directly. "Yes," he says, so soft I almost don't hear it. "I'm trying."

"Thank you." I swear to myself then and there, while I'm looking in his eyes, that I'll prove it to him. That he can trust me. That I can make things right. That I can take the real world and make it better. I lift a branch aside, and at last Eli follows me through the hedge.

There's a long silence between us. But my plan keeps me moving, quickly. Very soon people will be on these trails. If we're caught, there are going to be a lot of questions.

I trudge onto the new path, rolling my bike beside me. Ahead, skyscrapers sparkle with lights. On our left, the white gravestones of soldiers gleam in Arlington Cemetery under a predawn glow. They stretch on and on, as far as I can see. We climb a hill, then dip back down, then climb another. Finally, I spot the Iwo Jima Memorial ahead—a statue of a group of men bent over, holding an American flag. I start to scan the area for any apartments, but it's hard to see with trees everywhere.

"There." Eli points to something pale between the leaves.

We cross through the park. My feet throb and my bones ache. Wonder Dog ambles with her head down and her tail between her legs. Eli lumbers a few steps behind, like a zombie.

When we emerge from the trees, there's a big white apartment building right in front of us. And on the second floor, on an otherwise ordinary window, there are stickers. Superman stickers. Kenny.

I pull Eli with me across the street, then search for something to throw. I find a stick and chuck it at the window. It falls before it gets even halfway there.

Wonder Dog shoots me an unimpressed look.

"Are there any pebbles around or something?" I ask no one in particular, examining the ground.

Eli takes a protein bar out of his hoodie pocket. "Maybe try a chunk of this?"

I break off a pebble-sized bite and squish it into a circle. Then I throw it at the window. On my second protein-ball attempt, I actually hit the glass. But it takes five more tries before the blinds finally lift.

A bleary-eyed Kenny peers out the window at us. He blinks. Rubs his face. Looks again. I lift my hand and wave enthusiastically, miming, *Come outside!*

He gapes.

My arms start to get tired. Is he just going to gawk all day?

But no sooner do I think it than he moves away from the

window. For a moment, I worry he's gone for his dad—or just gone back to bed. Then the front door swings open, and Kenny comes out, dressed in sweatpants and a bright green T-shirt. His dirty-blond hair sticks up in random directions, like he's been electrocuted.

"What . . . ?" He's still staring with eyes the size of baseballs.

"Eli, can you watch Wonder Dog?" I ask, practically throwing my bike at him and dragging Kenny a few steps away. If Eli's still thinking about bolting, I don't want him getting too many weird vibes from Kenny.

Once we're out of Eli's hearing, I launch into an update on everything. About how yesterday—was it only yesterday?—at the Newseum I figured out Eli was a human trafficking victim. About how the police didn't help and my parents were not happy and now Eli's hurt and I'm trying to find my aunt Lexie.

Kenny's mouth drops farther and farther open the longer I talk. By the end of it all, I could stick an entire hamburger in it without even straining his jaw.

I expect him to argue that Eli couldn't possibly be a slave, or about how my imagination has gone haywire, but instead, he says, "You made him bike all the way here from your house while he's hurt?"

"What?" My face gets hot. "I didn't have a choice! Just— look."

I motion toward Eli. He's drooped over the bike, like it's holding him up instead of vice versa, but his eyes are sharp and attentive, darting from us to the windows to the street. When Wonder Dog nuzzles Eli's hand, he jumps and winces.

"He wanted to go on his own—find his mom by himself. The only person he trusts is me, Paddle—Wi-Fi—Kenny. Me and you. And I barely even got him to come here." I push my braids over my shoulder. "I've convinced him that we need my aunt, but if I do anything unexpected, he might freak and run off. So this is the way it has to be. Are you going to help or not?"

"Are you crazy?" Kenny glances at me and Eli and back at me. "Of course I'm gonna help. What do you need me to do?"

A smile tugs on my lips. "Okay, first—do you have your phone?"

Kenny pulls it out of his pocket. Together, we search for Aunt Lexie. One of the first results is a bio on a fancy law-yer website. The name of her organization is right at the top, and it takes only a few more taps before we have the address. I copy it down in my notepad.

"One more thing," I add. "Do you have a metro card we can borrow?"

Kenny shakes his head. "Not on me, but my dad keeps them in a bowl by the door."

I nod. "Can you get two? Then Eli and I will metro into DC."

"You can't take Wonder Dog on the train." He frowns, walking back over to Eli. "I'll put her inside. Your bike, too. She won't pee on my dad's carpet, right?"

I glare at him. "She only pees on the carpets of people who ask dumb questions."

"Got it." Kenny glances at Eli, who pushes the bike toward us with a nod. Kenny wheels it to the door, and Wonder has to follow. She looks back and whimpers.

Eli hurries after them and kneels to let Wonder lick his face. A faint smile turns up the corners of his mouth.

"It'll be okay," he murmurs. "Goodbye for now."

When Eli lets Wonder go, Kenny takes my dog by the harness and pulls her inside. Eli stands and moves beside me. A few minutes pass before Kenny returns, holding three cards and his phone. "I'm coming, too." He passes a card to me and one to Eli. "I mean—if that's okay."

I glance at Eli. He glances at me.

"If it's all right with you, Lightning Lane," he says, "it's all right with me."

"Then it's settled, Invisible Boy." I assume a heroic pose

with my fists on my hips. "The backyard birdhouse heroes unite once more."

"We're going to need to work on that name." Kenny grins. "Come on, Rosslyn Metro Station is this way."

Fifteen minutes later, we're on a train heading for the city. Kenny and I sit awkwardly in one row, and Eli collapses in the one behind us. He leans against the window and closes his eyes. Our car is about halfway filled with adults in business clothes, probably all early commuters. Some of them watch us curiously, but no one seems to particularly care about three kids alone on the train. I guess we've passed suspicious o'clock, but I'm not sure what time it actually is.

"So . . ." I shift in my seat and glance at Kenny. "You believe me?"

Kenny nods slowly. He whispers, "There's always been something . . . kind of off about him. It's hard to believe, but it makes sense. In a weird way."

I nod. I'll take that.

The train stops at a station and more people get on. Kenny waits until we're in motion again, then says, "So, how are we going to find his mom?"

"Well, he has a picture of her house."

"Can I see it?" Kenny asks.

I open my mouth to say probably not, but then a hand holds the photo out between our faces.

"Here," Eli mumbles. As soon as Kenny takes it, Eli flops back down on his seat and throws an arm over his eyes. I smile at him.

"Um. Thanks." Kenny turns over the picture and studies it. He sits up straighter, holding it closer.

I shift to face him. "What? Do you recognize it?"

"I—I don't know. Maybe." Kenny fishes out his phone and snaps a picture of the photo, but then he slumps again. "No signal. But I'll text my dad. It looks really, *really* familiar."

My heart thuds. "Seriously?"

He nods, typing with his thumbs while he shoots a grin at me. "Seriously maybe."

I take the photo and lean over the back of our seat, tucking it under the arm Eli has resting on his stomach. He's breathing heavily. Asleep. Maybe that's just as well—I don't want to raise his hopes again until we absolutely have a solid lead. I twist and sit down.

A few more stops go by. I fidget with the end of one braid. Kenny keeps checking his phone to see if the signal has gotten better. Two weeks ago, I would never have suspected Paddle Boy would be the person I need to save the day. And, as a reporter obligated to acknowledge the truth, I have to admit my instincts were off in this case.

"Look, ah—Kenny." I make myself take a deep breath. "I'm sorry about the whole—Paddle Boy thing. About holding it against you and never asking about it or whatever. That was kind of unfair."

He glances at me, surprised.

Part of me still wants to see a supervillain when I look at him. After all, an archenemy is fabulous material for a story. But I have to be willing to see what's actually right in front of me.

Anyway, in this case, a friend might be better.

"So, yeah." I sit up straighter. "I'm . . . glad you're in league with us."

Eli says, "Me too."

Kenny and I both jump.

"I thought you were asleep!" I squeak, turning. Eli still has his eyes closed.

"Invisible Boy never sleeps," he says sleepily.

"Well, it's a good thing you're awake." Kenny's face is bright red, but he points to the big metro map on the wall near us. "Because we're almost at our stop."

A few minutes later, we ride the long escalators out of

Smithsonian Station. As we come closer and closer to ground level, the purple-red sky grows bigger. I step off the escalator and move out of the way of the commuters, turning around in a circle to get my bearings.

The morning glows, streaking the lingering clouds in pink and teal. The National Mall stretches out on either side of me—green grass extending from the Capitol on my right to the Washington Monument on my left. A pale yellow sun peeks out over the buildings. Fingers of warm light touch everything from the monument's metal top to the pebbles at our feet. My lungs tighten.

"Wow," says Eli, beside me.

"Yeah," I whisper.

Even James couldn't capture this—this sunrise that somehow feels like it's happened for the very first time.

We made it. After everything, we made it.

Or—just about.

Taking a deep breath, I shake off the spell. "Okay. Kenny, can you map a route to my aunt's office?"

"Got it," Kenny says. In a second, the Google lady voice starts calmly giving us instructions.

Kenny takes the lead, heading away from the National Mall. I glance at his screen—6:02 a.m. Eli stays close to my side, casting uncertain looks at everyone. Commuters are out in force now. Traffic clogs the roads and crowds fill the sidewalks. We don't have anywhere to hide, but no one seems to notice us. Maybe they think we're on our way to summer school or something.

At the map's direction, we weave through streets. Kenny keeps his eyes down, often repeating the robot voice commands once or twice just to make sure we get them. I think about telling him that the ability to stop time hasn't damaged my hearing, but I decide after all the help he's giving us, I should hold it in. Besides, I'm too tired to care.

"It'll be on this next street," Kenny says, checking the instructions again. "We're almost—"

We step around the corner. My heart stops.

My parents are standing outside the building. With Aunt Lexie. And a policeman.

And Candace.

Chapter 22

THE TRUTH

I grab Kenny's and Eli's arms, but my feet stick to the pavement. It's too late.

"Nadia!" Mom shouts. "Get over here *right now*."

"Do you need me to cause a distraction?" Kenny asks in my ear. "I could jump into the street."

I shake my head. Getting hit by a car isn't going to help anyone. But my thoughts scatter as I search for a better idea. Questions crowd my brain. Like: *Why the heck are my parents with Candace? How did they know I'd come here?*

The policeman walks toward us. I glance at Eli, desperate. He drops his gaze to the ground. His skin has turned an ashy gray. In the morning light, the bruise on his cheek darkens.

The scab on his lip splits again when he breathes through his mouth. His hoodie hangs off one shoulder.

He didn't want to do this. *I* convinced him to come to Aunt Lexie's office. And now he's been caught.

"Come on, kids," the cop says, in reach now. "Let's go."

"We haven't done anything wrong," I say, more to myself and my friends than the cop. It's true, and the truth unglues my feet. I tighten my hold on the boys and walk forward, Kenny on my left and Eli on my right. I give Eli's arm a gentle shake. "Keep your head up, Invisible Boy. It isn't over."

He just nods, once. I'm not sure if he's saying *yes, I'll keep hoping* or *yes, it is over.* I wish I really could stop time—freeze everyone right here and come up with a plan, or whisk Eli away to safety, or convince him that we have the power to face down a supervillain and win. With time on pause, I could explain everything to Mom and Dad. I could get them on my side before Candace twists the truth into a lie.

As we approach, I get a better view of my parents—and wish I'd been studying the pavement like Eli. Bright red crying blotches cover Mom's face. Dad stands as still and pale as the marble wall behind him. Their clothes are rumpled, like they got dressed in the dark. Beside them, Aunt Lexie clasps and unclasps her hands, casting worried looks between me and my parents. She's the only one dressed nicely, but even she just has her hair back in a loose ponytail, as if she left the house in a rush.

My stomach turns over. I didn't even think about how worried they would be.

Candace leans on my mom's arm weakly. She has dark circles under her eyes and her hair whirls around her head like a tangled hat. Nothing like the perfect-neighbor act. Her face is red, too, like she's been crying. Mom squeezes her shoulder. I wish the cop would go ahead and slap handcuffs on Candace, but he stands back by his cruiser, watching without interfering.

I grip Eli's sleeve.

"What were you thinking, Nadia?" Mom half sobs, half whispers when we stop in front of them. She tries to hug me—which doesn't work too well, with my hands still clenched on the boys. I push Eli a little behind me, so I can shield him. "We were worried sick!"

"Eli, thank God," Candace whispers, wiping her eyes. "Ohh, just look at you! Are you hurt?"

"Kenny, what are you—?" my dad starts to ask. "How did you get pulled into—?"

Mom lets me go and tucks one wet braid behind my ear. "Are you okay?"

"I—" I have no idea how to answer that. So I move on to my own question. "H-how did you find us?"

"Candace came by the house at about three a.m. to say she thought you might have run off with her foster son—Eli?" Mom glances at him, but only for a millisecond, before she focuses on me again. "We thought you were in bed! But when we couldn't find—"

Her voice breaks. Dad puts a hand on her shoulder and rubs. "We remembered what Lexie had told you," he says. "So we guessed you might have . . . done something."

"We tried to call you, Dia." Aunt Lexie swallows, staying a few steps away to give my parents room. I wish she'd come closer, get between us and Candace. "I couldn't figure out why you weren't answering. Then your parents found your phone on your bed . . ."

I lift my chin, looking past my mom and straight at my aunt. With all the strength I can muster, I say, "Eli is a slave. A"—I search for the exact term Aunt Lexie used before—"domestic servant."

My parents glance at Candace, and she shakes her head, mouth agape. "I—I—" She shifts her gaze to Eli and reaches for him. "Honey, are you okay? What happened?"

I pull him nearer, so she can't touch him. To Aunt Lexie, I keep talking. "I've seen where he sleeps—in a basement closet, on lumpy pillows and a sleeping bag. I've seen all the stuff he does—working in the yard every day for hours."

"I saw that part, too," Kenny says, raising a hand.

"And *yeah*, he's hurt." I point to the bruise on Eli's cheek. "Because *she* did this!"

"How could you say such things?" Candace asks, voice fragile as glass. "If this is another game, it's gone too far. Just look at you, Eli—did you fall on your way here?" She holds out her arms again. "Sweetie, let me see those scrapes."

"Are you sure this lady is a trafficker?" Kenny whispers to me.

"I know what I saw," I say, louder. Maybe I would have doubted it at another time, but not now. "I know what he said. Right?" I turn to Eli. "Right?"

"What on earth did you tell this poor girl, Eli?" Candace wipes her cheeks, but immediately fresh tears gather in her eyes. She looks over her shoulder at Aunt Lexie and my parents. "I took him from an abusive father and brought him into my home. I've been doing my best with him—but he's a troubled kid. Sometimes I'm not sure he's entirely . . . I think he imagines things. Like your daughter."

I concentrate on breathing. Eli doesn't move or speak. He stares down at his shoes.

"Nadia," Mom says, confused but gentle, "you can let him go. You're all safe. There must be some misunderstanding . . ."

"Lexie, you're the expert," Dad says to her. "Tell Nadia that he's fine."

Aunt Lexie opens and closes her mouth. "It—isn't that simple."

Everyone starts talking at once.

Dad says, "What do you mean?"

Mom says, "We need to get you kids into some dry clothes."

Candace leans forward and takes Eli's shoulder, like she's going to pull him into a hug. "Come on, dear. Let me—"

Eli doesn't resist. His eyes are going dim. His shoulders are slumping.

I hold on to him and yell in Candace's face, "NO."

The adults freeze, staring at me.

The cop takes a step forward.

"Get. Your. Hands. Off. Him." My voice has taken on a life of its own. My head goes completely silent, and I know nothing and feel nothing except that if she doesn't let go of Eli right now, I'm going to lose it.

Candace is facing me, so I'm the only one who notices her eyes harden. A tear wavers on her eyelash, but doesn't fall. Low, so low my parents might not even hear it, she says,

"Don't let your imagination run away with you, now. This isn't a time for games."

My body goes cold, and she doesn't need heat vision to burn a hole through me.

Calm and quiet, a voice beside me says, "Don't speak to her like that."

"What?" Candace glances at Eli.

Eli lifts his head.

And he meets Candace's eyes.

Her skin pales and then flushes.

"*Stop*," she hisses. She doesn't blink. The tear drops. "Stop doing that."

Eli grips my hand. "No."

Aunt Lexie moves closer to us. She looks right at Eli.

And sees him.

Chapter 23

THE EXTRAORDINARY SECRET OF SUPERHEROES

Nadia's telling the truth." Eli never shifts his gaze from Candace, but I think he's talking to all of us. "For two years, I've been locked in a closet room in the basement at night. I cook and clean for parties. I take care of the gardens. I haven't been to school."

Candace's jaw goes slack. Then she pulls back her hand, like she might slap Eli. But before she can, Aunt Lexie catches her arm.

"None of that," she says to Candace. Then she looks over at the officer. "Can you hold this woman on suspicion of child abuse?"

The policeman nods, stepping around us to take her arm. Candace clenches her fists.

"You shouldn't be charging me with anything," she says to Aunt Lexie. "Can't you see the boy? He needs to go to a hospital. I need to take him to a hospital."

Aunt Lexie ignores her. "Eli, could I talk to you alone for a sec?"

Eli hesitates. I squeeze his hand.

"She's a good one," I whisper to him. "I promise, Invisible Boy. She's safe."

His mouth twitches, almost like a smile. "Okay, Lightning Lane."

I let him go and watch while he and Aunt Lexie move nearer the building. The cop hasn't handcuffed Candace, but he's standing near her while she talks in a quick, concerned sort of voice. Mom hasn't moved. Dad puts an arm around her waist. My body feels like wires are strung through me, holding me up, keeping me alert even though exhaustion clouds the corners of my brain.

Kenny nudges my side and I almost jump out of my skin. "I think I found her."

I blink. "Found who?"

"Eli's mom." Kenny holds out his phone. On the screen is a series of texts.

5:52 a.m.

hey do you recognize this house

Dad 6:10 a.m.

Why are you up at 5 looking at houses???

6:14 a.m.

Yeah I recognize it. It's on my running route by the Navy Yard.
Don't know the address, obv.

6:17 a.m.

Why?

6:21 a.m.

If you're actually awake, want to have breakfast together?

291

6:33 a.m.

Breakfast is ready. There's bacon.

6:38 a.m.

I've got to go to work soon, so last call for father-son breakfast bonding.

6:41 a.m.

Why is there a dog in your room???

6:42 a.m.

Where are you?!

6:45 a.m.

kinda busy
update soon
i'm fine

6:46 a.m.

Answer your phone!

"Oh my gosh." I look at Kenny, almost bursting with excitement. "Oh my gosh, this is amazing. This could be it!"

Kenny shrugs and smiles. "It's a pretty memorable house. See—here."

He leans over and switches to another window on his phone. It's a Google Street View image of a purple place in a row of town houses. And it looks exactly like Eli's mom's house in her picture. I squeak in excitement and throw my arms around Kenny.

"I'm so, so glad you aren't a supervillain!" I cry. "Thank you, thank you, thank you!"

Kenny starts to say several things at once and manages to say nothing intelligible.

I let him go and toss his phone back to him. "Call your dad and tell him everything before we get in even more trouble."

"Right, yeah." He's grinning from ear to ear as he steps away.

My mom edges toward me. My glee almost vanishes when I look at her sad, tired, worried face.

"Is the baby okay?" I blurt. "Aunt Lexie said you had problems with babies before and I didn't mean to worry you so much and—"

"Yes, yes." Mom wraps her arms around me. Softly, she

says into my hair, "I don't even know what to think right now, Nadia."

Dad joins her, putting his arm around us both.

"I'm sorry," I mumble into her shirt. "I just . . . didn't know what to do. And Eli needed me."

"I can't get over how risky this was," Mom murmurs. "You were in a lot of danger, Nadia. I don't think you even know how much."

"Helping him was the right thing to do." I tilt my head up and glance from her to Dad. "Doing what's right is more important than doing what's safe."

"I wish you had come to us," Dad says. He doesn't sound angry—just sad.

Tears gather in my eyes. In a tiny voice, I remind them, "I *did*."

"You did." Mom nods, and *she* starts crying again. "I'm so sorry, Nadia."

She pulls me close, and Dad tightens his hold around us. I lean against her and inhale the smell of laundry soap. Her belly has a small, hard bump. My little sister is in on the hug, too.

Aunt Lexie walks past us to the cop, and I lean toward them so I won't miss what happens next. Eli stands a bit away, but I wave him over and take his hand again.

"Please take down Ms. Goldenberry's information," Aunt Lexie tells the policeman, "and have her held for abuse of a minor."

Candace starts to protest, but Lexie just comes back to us.

Mom blinks. "He's really—?"

Aunt Lexie nods, once. "Further investigation will be necessary. But it seems likely." She looks at me. "I'd like to get your testimony, Nadia. Why don't we all go inside?"

We leave Candace with the cop, enter the building, and pile into the elevator—Kenny and Eli and me in one corner and the adults on the other side. It's quiet. Eli and I lean our shoulders together, almost too tired to stand.

On an upper floor, Aunt Lexie leads the way through a lobby area to a carpeted room with tables, coffee machines, and snacks.

"Karen, Richard, Kenny, please make yourselves comfortable here. I won't be gone too long." Aunt Lexie turns to Eli and me. "Eli, I'd like to introduce you to our in-house social worker. She will help figure out our next steps. And Nadia, we'll go to my office."

I give my parents and Kenny a wave. Kenny salutes back. Then Eli and I follow Aunt Lexie down the hall, first to a lady Aunt Lexie calls Ms. Kyley, where we leave Eli, and then to Aunt Lexie's own room. It has a wall of floor-to-ceiling bookshelves and a big desk covered in neatly arranged piles of papers. Aunt Lexie sinks into a bright green armchair and waves me to a small couch by the bookshelf. She takes out a notepad—one that's not too different from mine.

"Okay, Girl Reporter," Aunt Lexie says, a smile quirking the corners of her mouth, "what's the scoop?"

———— /////////// ————

After I finish, Aunt Lexie takes me to a conference room. "I need to talk to your parents and get the information on Eli's mom's house from Kenny," she says, her hand on the doorknob. "You did the right thing, Nadia. But if you ever have a suspicion again, you talk to me—or call a human trafficking hotline and make a report. Promise?"

"Oh, sure," I reply. "What's a hotline?"

"It's a phone number for experts. You have no idea how dangerous . . ." She shakes her head and sighs. "Never mind. I'm sorry I wasn't there when you needed me."

"It's okay." I give Aunt Lexie a hug. Her fresh-paper smell

wraps around me like a shield, and I start to relax when I remember—"How was the *movie*?"

Aunt Lexie actually *blushes*. "Nice."

"Did you set a date for your wedding?" I grin. "Is he going to shoot it himself, even though he's the groom?"

"Hey, don't push it." She pokes me in the shoulder. "I refuse to be controlled by a matchmaker. And *if*, *someday*, in the *very far future*, there *happened* to be a wedding—anyone who teases me will be wearing the ugliest bridesmaid dress money can buy. I'm thinking . . . hot pink?"

I stick out my tongue. She sticks hers out right back.

"Get some rest, wild child. And"—she pushes the door open—"for the record, I think you're going to put Lois Lane to shame."

I snort. I have a long way to go before I'm even *close*.

Aunt Lexie shuts the door behind her. I wander over to a side table against the wall with snacks set out in baskets and canned sodas cooling in bowls of ice. I take a packet of pretzels and another of crackers, plus a candy bar and a can of Coke. The breakfast of champions.

There's a long, fancy table down the center of the room with a ton of chairs and a huge TV at the far end. The wall near me is glass, facing the hallway, but the far wall is a floor-to-ceiling window of the Washington skyline. I step around the table to get a better look.

Eli's sitting on the floor, legs crossed. He glances at me and swallows a mouthful of food. "Hi."

At this point, I'm so used to him just appearing out of nowhere I don't even feel that surprised. I plop down next to him, taking note of the scattered chip bags and chocolate bar wrappers. He's helped himself to the snack table, too.

"How're you doing?" I ask, tearing my pretzels open.

"Fine." He shrugs. "Ms. Kyley is going to have someone take me to the hospital, so I can get checked out. But I think I'm all right."

A new bandage peeks from under the hole in his jeans around his knee. I hold out my pretzels. He accepts a few and munches quietly.

"Aunt Lexie said they'll put you in a home for a little while," I say to Eli. "Just until they can check on stuff with your mom."

He nods. "Ms. Kyley told me. It's fine," he adds, glancing at me. "You promised to help me find my mom, and you have. It's just going to take longer than either of us thought."

"Yeah," I agree, disappointment stinging my throat.

"But there's something good." Eli brightens. He actually almost smiles. "Ms. Kyley said the home provides tutors who can help me start catching up on school."

I try very hard not to make a face. "You have to do summer school?"

"I *get* to do summer school." Now he is actually grinning. "Got to start somewhere."

I shrug, returning his smile. "I guess."

We both look out at the city. Far to the left, there's the Washington Monument. Far to the right, the Capitol building. Tourists and traffic bustle through the streets, but all of it feels distant right now. Like we're watching from our very own secret lair. A hideout where we can spy on the city and swoop down to the rescue.

"Thanks, by the way."

I turn to Eli, my mouth full of pretzels. "Hmm?"

"For helping."

"Oh. Yeah, no prob."

The sun shines through the window, warm on my skin and fizzling in the air around me. Part of me wants to flop down and go to sleep right here. I rub my palm on the bristly carpet. Dark and light blue interwoven together. Flecks of dust spring up around my hand and twirl in the light. I try to take in all the details. I need to record them later.

We sit shoulder to shoulder, and I wonder what will happen to Eli. Where he'll live and what friends he'll make and what kind of teacher he'll be when he grows up. I wonder when we'll just sit together in the sun, like this, again.

There's so much to say and nothing to say at the same time. And in a few minutes, the door will open, and we'll be pulled back into the real world.

But for now, we sit, disguised in our secret identities as normal kids.

I know the truth, though.

We're a superhero and his ace reporter.

The Alexandria Tribune

Winner of the Junior Journalists Contest Award

Local Girl Wins Journalism Award for Article "Stop Human Trafficking Right Where You Are" by Nadia Quick

EDITOR'S NOTE: The following article received first place in the Junior Journalists Contest, and is reprinted below with permission from Junior Journalists Inc.

My name is Nadia Quick, and I believed that a supervillain lived on my street. In a way, I was right.

Not every villain wears a mask or a cape. Sometimes they look like ordinary neighbors. On Stratford Lane in Alexandria, Va., that ordinary-looking woman was Candace Goldenberry, a pharmacist, socialite, and alleged human trafficker.

Human trafficking is the term used for modern-day slavery. According to the organization Love149, human trafficking always involves one or more of the following factors: force, fraud, or coercion. *Force* might mean that the trafficked person has to perform acts in order to survive (for instance, to get food or shelter). *Fraud* could be a debt held over the head of the victim—normally one that is impossible to pay off. *Coercion* might look like threats if a person does not obey.

It is estimated that there are over five million children trafficked around the world. In Virginia alone, from 2012 to 2016 there were about seven hundred cases reported that involved almost 1500 individual people. The most common type of labor trafficking in Virginia is domestic servitude. But statistics can't possibly capture the entire picture, because no one really knows how much human trafficking is going on. The whole point of it is to be a secret. The best way to learn more is to listen to the stories of the people who escape.

Goldenberry is in an ongoing investigation involving a minor, whose name cannot be disclosed here. I will be calling him Clark Kent for the purposes of confidentiality.

Kent (14) was given to Goldenberry by his father, who owed the alleged trafficker a substantial amount of money for pharmaceutical drugs she had illegally sold to him. Kent worked for Goldenberry for over two years as a domestic servant, maintaining her house and catering for parties. He escaped with help from two friends and has begun the long road to recovery and reintegration, which is a fancy way of saying he's learning how to be a kid again.

"First, I was placed in a safe home," Kent told me. "It wasn't bad—I was kind of nervous, but the house was clean and the adults were nice. We—me and the other kids—had a pretty strict schedule, but I liked that. While my social worker got in touch with my mom, I attended a summer school to catch up on the classes I'd missed."

By the end of the summer, Kent reached the seventh-grade learning level. He now lives with his mother and attends school near her home.

"It isn't exactly the way I dreamed," he says with a smile. "I still see counselors a lot. But I am happy."

Social workers and others caution that it will be a long journey for Kent, as it is for others like him. Everyone's transition out of human trafficking looks different, and all of it is very complicated. Kent is lucky because he has support from lawyers, social workers, neighbors, and two super-amazing friends.

"Cases like [Kent]'s are not unusual," lawyer Alexandria Miller commented, "but every situation is unique.

"There is hope," she adds. "The more people who can recognize trafficking, the better chance we have to help survivors. And people—especially kids—are astounding. In the most difficult circumstances, they survive. Give them a safe place, with plenty of love and friends and support, and they thrive. [Kent] is already well on his way there."

Trafficking can look very different depending on the

type and the people involved, but according to Polaris (a leading research organization for human trafficking) there are a few universal signs, broadly grouped into: abnormal behavior, poor physical health, and lack of control. More specifically, the individual in question:

- Is not free to come or go at will
- Is under eighteen and providing adult services
- Is unpaid, paid very little, or paid only through tips
- Works excessively long and/or unusual hours
- Encounters high-security measures in work and/or living locations (e.g., boarded-up windows, privacy fences, security cameras, etc.)
- Is fearful, anxious, depressed, submissive, tense, or nervous/paranoid
- Exhibits unusually fearful or anxious behavior when confronted with law enforcement or immigration officials
- Shows signs of poor hygiene, malnourishment, and/or fatigue
- Has few or no personal possessions
- Is not allowed or able to speak for themselves (a third party may insist on being present)
- Shares scripted, confusing, or inconsistent stories

- Protects the person who may be hurting them or minimizes abuse

The crime of human trafficking is far from invisible, but most people don't know or refuse to notice the signs. Kids like Kent are all around us. Maybe in your own neighborhood. What will you choose to see?

If you suspect someone is being human trafficked, call or text the National Human Trafficking Hotline: 1 (888) 373-7888 / SMS: 233733 (Text HELP or INFO)

Nadia Quick, 13, hopes to one day be a journalist, and already has a lead on developing news: An international photographer and a crime-fighting lawyer have joined forces and may be moving toward a till-death-do-us-part union. Nadia loves canoeing with friends, Superman comics, and her baby sister, Lucy. She looks forward to being the next Lois Lane.

AUTHOR'S NOTE

LONDON, November 2014—I am at the Trust Conference, surrounded by people from all over the world who have one big reason to be here: We all want to stop human trafficking. It's an odd mix of lawyers, volunteers, researchers, fancy donors, and international non-government workers. In the lobby during a break, I stand in a corner and clutch my cup of tea and just watch. These are some of the most passionate, lionhearted people in the world. Dozens of languages swirl around me. It is as overwhelming as it is wonderful.

I have never stared down terrorists to save child soldiers. I have never crawled through mica mines searching for a friend. I have never counseled girls who were rescued, only to be rejected by their hometowns. I am fresh out of university, a writer without a book, and all I have to offer is my anger and my desire to act.

I stand in the corner and ask myself, *How does a writer for young people enter this conversation?*

And the answer seems obvious—a writer writes.

VIRGINIA, February 2018—I am attending one of the advocacy classes at the Virginia Beach Justice Initiative, an organization in my area that specializes in identifying and helping trafficking victims. Years of study mean I'm hardly shocked when I learn that this area is one of the biggest hubs for human trafficking in the USA. We are a port city with a high military population—two things that often indicate human trafficking will be close by.

But then my teachers tell me about an investigation of a local business. A business I know, because it's across the parking lot from my doctor's office. A business where women came and went, and instead of making a report, the employees next door made jokes. Because it couldn't possibly be human trafficking. Not here. Not in front of them.

Except it was.

I tell this story to students and friends, and the response is almost always the same: "*Here?*" Then they think about it and tell me what they've seen—shabbily dressed girls with well-dressed men at movie theaters, or waitresses who are removed after you ask where they're from, or hotel staff with barcodes tattooed on their necks. And I say, "*Yes, here.*"

Trafficking happens in every part of America—city, rural, suburban, north, south, east, and west. It can take place around big events—like an election, Super Bowl, or World Cup—and it can take place in the ordinary workings of a neighborhood. Trafficked people can be found in hotels, restaurants, houses, and many other locations you might never think to look.

And that's the hardest part: seeing.

VIRGINIA, Summer 2020—This has been the most difficult story I have ever had to write. The hardest conversation I've ever tried to enter. Because, honestly, everyone—even me—chooses not to see sometimes.

This book touches on only one type of trafficking, but there are many different forms it can take. Every survivor's story is unique and worthy of being heard. Though Eli is fictional, his situation was heavily influenced by testimonies I heard and read. And though Nadia is made up, she is very much based on my own personality. I'd rather invent whimsical tales than see the truth sometimes, and in doing that, I fail to use my power for good. Stories can make the world better, but only if you know the truth first.

Make the difficult choice. When something seems odd, don't talk yourself out of it right away. Speak to an adult you trust. Find out if they notice the same things. And even if you aren't completely sure, you can always text, call, or email the National Human Trafficking Hotline to let a professional know you're concerned.

Human trafficking is scary. But we all have our own Smallville, Metropolis, or Gotham—places we know better than anyone else. Maybe you can enter a garden no one else thinks exists. Maybe you go to school with a kid no one else seems to notice. Maybe you listen to conversations no one else seems to hear.

Seek the truth, and you'll uncover your own super-power.

You'll be able to see.

ACKNOWLEDGMENTS

This book, y'all. This book. Where do I even begin?

Kate and Fliss, my intrepid editors: Thank you for always believing I could pull it off, even when I wasn't so sure. Thank you for pushing me to do my best. Amber, my super literary agent: Thank you for the many pep talks and encouraging words when I was a puddle of doubt. This book would absolutely, positively not exist without the three of you.

Thank you to Deborah Lee for her wonderful cover and illustrations. I'll be staring at this art for a long time to come!

To my early readers: Amelia Todd, Anna Gibson, Jenny Smith, and many more. Thank you for bringing your expertise to the pages!

Lora Innes, who first introduced me to the phrase *human trafficking* and to Love146: Thank you for using your unique gifts to enter the conversation. Bet you didn't realize you'd be pulling me in, too.

The Thomson Reuters Foundation and Trust Conference: Your work is truly an inspiration. My deep gratitude especially to these speakers, who redefined my understanding of so much: Deependra Giri, Evelyn Chumbow, Kailash Satyarthi, Chaker Khazaal, and Monique Villa. To Jennifer Kempton, who I spoke to about this project days before the end, and who will always remind me that trauma doesn't disappear when you're freed.

To the Virginia Beach Justice Initiative: Your advocacy class was one of the most challenging and growing experiences of my life. I am in awe of the work you do on local, state, and national levels. God bless you and your girls.

To Paddle Boy: You probably don't even know that's your name, but if you were a preteen boy living on Wakefield Street in 2002–2003 and you once wandered into someone's yard and smashed their canoe paddle on a tree and then ran in the other direction when the father of the house came out to chase you down, I am still waiting for my replacement paddle. Feel free to get in touch via my publicist.

To my friends and family (notable exception: Paddle Boy): There are too many of you to name, but you know who you are. Thanks for celebrating the highs and patiently patting me through the angst. Especially Mom, who probably had more than her fair share of counseling me through the rough patches.

And to the one who sees every face, every tear, every smile: Christ Jesus. Teach me to leave no one invisible.